oons from Carl

R. hide my bubble gum
n my secret food
rner

de my pocket knife
my hollow book

t more atomic
balls for the big
TO SELL

S.M.C. is really mean
And her legs she never

P9-BIR-632

Caveman Caves

n my lis
But so are
And of cour

My brother at
And man that
He hogs the best
I'll tell my mom

I put some dog f
In my big brother's
I think I heard him
With the dogs he was

I want to meet old Snoopy Brown
That's Charlie's little dog
He looks kind of like Frisky
Who is my potato chip hog
I called him that because today
Frisky did something so bad
He stole a bag of potato chips
From my poor old dad
Dad went out to the picnic table
To have a shady lunch
And when he came back the bag was gone
Frisky ate the whole chip bunch
So I think Snoopy Brown, because he's
so smart
Could help my dog be good
Tonight he has to sleep in the garage
I'll sneak out with my sleeping bag.
yeah, I really should!

duh!
Eye tuk
Eye don't
Becuz
think i

Joe Cool

POP
RPLOP

with a
but I
om took
th, but I
maybe he

ed in

city and the snow

from
pond

e bees &
this

e out how to
I need a new
e in BUT

Today Carl was bothering me
He does that every day
I'm going to put ants in his bed
By mom will say no way
So I'll put them in his backpac
For his Boy Scout sleep out
All those ants will creep out
And give his butt a bite

BATWOMEN
S.M.C. and others are
dressed up all in black
I know at night that they
can fly and their students
they'll attack
But if they ever come near
me, I'll get them really good
I'll call out from the forest
the evil Man in the WOOD
looooohhhaaaah

THE WORLD ACCORDING TO GABE

(More stories from the upper bunk)

Book 2

in the Go Ask Mom series

Written by
JUSTIN MATOTT

Illustrations by
LISA TARR

To Ms. Linden
Enjoy!

DISCLAIMER

As in the first book in this series, this book was written about a time prior to this day and age with its obsessive concern about political correctness. There is nothing in this book that is intended to be offensive to any ethnic or gender group, or to zombies, nuns, Catholics, crazy old ladies, mean big brothers, snotty rich people, teachers, or even lobsters or "mudbugs." However, there is dialogue and subject matter that may be offensive to the overly prim and proper. Mr. Matott takes full responsibility for being disgusting at times, and for writing a book that a child, be they young or older than young, will actually enjoy reading. Relax, read, enjoy!

By the way, dear librarian and teacher friends, Mr. Matott suggests reading this book privately before reading it as a read-aloud. You might risk a bit of disruptive laughter and a few "gas" jokes as a result if you don't heed this advice.

THE WORLD ACCORDING TO GABE

Text copyright © 2009 by JUSTIN MATOTT
Illustrations copyright © 2009 by Lisa M. Tarr
Jacket design by Laurie McAdam

All rights reserved under International and Pan-American Copyright Conventions.
No part of this publication may be reproduced or transmitted in any form or by any means, electronic or mechanical, including photocopy, recording, or any information storage and retrieval system, without permission in writing from the publisher.
Requests for permission to make copies of any part of the work should be mailed to:
Permissions Department, SKOOB BOOKS,
P. O. Box 261183 Littleton, CO 80163.
Library of Congress Cataloging-in-Publication Data
Go Ask Mom! written by JUSTIN MATOTT.;
illustrated by Lisa Tarr – 1st ed. p. cm.
Summary: A young man and his band of brothers find great adventures in a world according to them.
ISBN 1-889191-20-5 {1. chapter book series. I. Lisa Tarr –ill. II. Title First edition
A B C D E
To contact JUSTIN MATOTT regarding his work, please see his website at
www.justinmatott.com.
For LISA TARR please see her website at www.tarrart.com.
Printed in Canada.

DEDICATION

Gabriel Peters is a fictitious character in a fictitious book, who just happens to be borrowing some of the not so fictitious aspects of a certain author's life.

I met my first real life enemy in my first year as a fourth grader. Her name was not actually Sister Mary Claire but something quite similar. She was possibly one of the meanest and most disliked teachers I've known. Her methods of humiliation and put-downs weren't lost on me. I was the smallest boy in the class (due to the fact that I had been advanced two grades past my peers, like Gabriel), I walked with a limp (I had a bent bone in my right leg, creating the need to wear a built up shoe) and I was disruptive in class (I was very nearsighted and could not read the blackboard or anything that wasn't within inches of my face.) Nevertheless, Sister Mary Claire seemed to take great delight in making me feel about two inches small and showed little empathy for a struggling little boy who just wanted to fit in and more than anything not stick out. SO, IT IS FOR ALL OF THE TEACHERS WHO STRIVE TO BE DIFFERENT THAN THIS AND MAKE A POSITIVE DIFFERENCE IN HER OR HIS STUDENT'S LIVES THAT I DEDICATE THIS BOOK.

To Andy Kamlet and Les Anderson. If we'd been boys together we'd have had a blast! - To Mark Lehnertz at The Tattered Cover Book Store, thank you for making it a 'habit' to sort out the 'wimples'! - To Jason Tarr, for helping me to find the right name for this book. -
J. Matott
To Chris, Jason, Sydney & Snoopy: my best friends, biggest fans, most honest critics and the most incredible family that one could ever dream of. ILY - L. Tarr

3

CONTENTS

PROLOGUE

In the last week of summer, Mom and Dad walked out of my room with the saddest looks on their faces. I could tell they felt almost as bad as I did.

My brother Carl stood in my doorway with a look of astonishment on his face, having overheard our conversation. He then just shook his head and crept back to his room.

"WHAT??" I screamed after my departing folks. "WHAT? NO WAY! I cannot repeat fourth grade! I cannot, I cannot! You promised that I was going to change schools!" THIS ISN'T FAIR AT ALL!

I then screamed into my pillow at the top of my lungs. It was bad enough to think about being a repeater and all the kids who would make fun of me, but the worse part was that I was going to have to repeat classes with Sister Mary Claire. Mom had talked to me about repeating fourth grade at Pioneer Ridge Elementary School instead, the same public school everyone else in Skyview, our neighborhood, goes to, and that was bad enough, but now it was the worst news ever, repeating in my old school AND in the same class with the same dumb old teacher! That was simply more than I could take. Even though Mom had explained over and over that I would graduate from High School several years younger than all of the other kids and then it would really matter to me, I didn't care. IT JUST ISN'T FAIR AT ALL!

My first fourth-grade year had been a nightmare in many ways. At least my eye patch was coming off before school began and my leg was a lot better that it used to be. But how could they promise me that I was going to get out of St. Joseph's and then go back on their word?

As I said, Mom and Dad had tried to explain that there were real reasons that I was going to stay at St. Joe's. Maybe their reasons made sense to them, but I was the one who had to stay. Since I didn't want to hear their reasons, I didn't really listen to them; after all, they had promised me that I would be going to Prairie Vista Elementary and now it wasn't going to happen.

I wanted to run away from home.

My friends went to the normal school, the public school with the big yellow bus that squeaked loudly in the early morning as it rounded the corner and headed up Venus Avenue toward my house to pick the kids up at the bus stop. I always wanted to ride that bus with the other kids, including my big brother, but instead I rode in the carpool of misfits, us kids who for a bunch of reasons didn't fit into the normal scheme of things and didn't go to the same school as all of the other kids in the neighborhood.

My carpool had these twin sisters with poodle-puff blond hair and breath that always smelled like raspberry Kool-Aid, and a boy named Ike who never talked to anyone in the car but stared out his window, singing to himself and ignoring everyone else in the car. Sometimes this other boy named Bhasin with really dark skin who came from India rode with us when his mom couldn't take him to St. Joe's because she had to take care of his sick sister. I always felt sorry for that kid, because he never got any attention on account of his sister. He seemed really sad. Then there was of course me, the clown of the car as Mrs. Abernathy called me, but everyone knew I went to the Catholic school* because I was smart and needed a challenge.

*Catholic school (noun), a private school supported by a particular church or parish.

It seemed to me like just going to the school and surviving the day was the real challenge!

The moms took turns driving us back and forth downtown to the school. I didn't like it when the little Indian kid's mom drove because she had this rickety old brown station wagon that barely made it every time (we broke down on the side of the road two times already in the first month of my fourth-grade year), and she smoked like a train.

Whenever I hear that saying, "...smokes like a train," it always makes me think of *The Little Engine That Could* and how if he smoked he couldn't have gotten up that hill because he would be all out of breath and really blue in the face. Come to think of it, he was blue in the face, and blue all over for that matter.

I was always doing stuff like that, daydreaming and thinking about stuff in a weird way. My dad just said it was because I live in my head, in my imagination, and that it is a good thing. Everyone else just seems to think I am strange.

As I said before, I wanted to ride the big yellow school bus with the other kids from my neighborhood. It got so bad that one day I just hopped on the bus after my brother got on. It was kind of sad, because my mom got really scared and called the police when I wasn't around to get in the carpool. I hid under a seat all the way to the public school, that I only got to go to when my brother's class had a play or the annual school carnival.

My mom and dad told me that they had imagined all kinds of crazy stuff happening to me while I was missing. It was like I was one of those kids on the posters who show up every so often in the post office or on the side of a milk carton: HAVE YOU SEEN ME?

Geez, I wasn't ever really missing! My brother was only three feet away from me the whole time, but no one saw me get on the bus because the bus driver was on the tetherball court flirting with the weird divorced lady who had no kids at the school, but was always standing out there near the bus stop in a fancy dress and tons of makeup. I guess she liked the bus driver or something.

When all of the kids went to their classes I wandered into the library and started reading one of *The Happy Hollisters* mystery books. The librarian finally saw me sitting on the floor in the back and then took me to the office, where my mom was called.

I was sent home in the janitor's car. He told me all kinds of funny stories about pranks he pulled on other people when he was a boy. He had gone to a Catholic school too, and had some funny stories about it.

When I got home my mom hugged me so hard that I thought my brain was going to pop out. She then drove me over to St. Joe's and walked me into my fourth grade class. That's kind of embarrassing in a way, but it made me feel kind of special, too.

When I got home later that day, the kids at the bus stop were talking about my stunt.

Well, all of this to say that going to the Catholic school in a uniform every day, when almost all of the other kids in my neighborhood are in the yellow school bus in their jeans and t-shirts, has singled me out. When we all play hide-n-seek or some other game and they started talk about stuff that happened at their school, I always feel left out. I like the summers best, because no one goes to school, and after just a few weeks they all stop talking about stuff at school and we are all the same for a little while.

One thing I did this past year, that my brother said was sissy, was to keep a diary. I liked it. I liked having an imaginary friend who heard all of my stories, shared all of my inner secrets. Something about writing it all down for me was like getting it all out. Like throwing up when you feel really lousy. My diary was a place to go throw it all up. I have a lot to throw up too, because for a little kid, I have already been through a ton of rough stuff.

So, the bottom line is there is nothing I can do about repeating fourth grade again. Besides, if I don't I will barely be a teenager when I graduate from high school because I skipped both second and third grades, no lie, and that will make me even more of a misfit than I am now. So, like it or not, as my big brother Carl and his friends will say over and over, "Gabriel Peters is going to fourth grade AGAIN! GABRIEL PETERS IS A REPEATER!" This year is going to be a waste! I already learned everything there was to know in fourth grade last year. I thought they said I was so smart. Maybe they had it all wrong?

Now I only have a few more weeks of freedom left to do all the things kids like to do before I am back in the Batwoman's torture chamber. I just cannot believe I am going to have to repeat Sister Mary Claire. Trust me, repeating any grade is bad enough without having to repeat her! DANG! DANG! DANG!

So, the stuff you are about to read is from my diaries. I like telling stories, and keeping the diaries helps me to remember details. Stories about your life and junk always seem to be better when you tell them later, after it has happened and having some of the nitty-gritty details makes a story so much better! I really only want to tell you about the summertime, because summertime is the best time of the whole year, but some interesting things happened in my second fourth grade year that made me look forward to the next summer even more, so here goes....

CHAPTER ONE

Blue Streaks

I always thought that if Sister Mary Claire, my meanest teacher ever, weren't married to Jesus, she would have cussed me out every day at school. Good thing I have a little while left before I have to deal with her again!

She doesn't like me that much, for some reason. The truth is, she doesn't seem to like any of the boys in my class. She is always ignoring us when we raise our hands to answer questions and almost always favors the girls: "BOYS, SIT STILL! BOYS, BE QUIET! BOYS, BE NICE!" Just once I'd like to hear her call the girls down.

I bet she is a secret cusser when she isn't around kids, just like Old Man Stoltz, who lives down the street. He doesn't like any of us kids in the neighborhood.

Old Man Stoltz is this funny old guy with a back bent like a comma. He has nasty hairs growing out of his ears and nose, and these funny black glasses that cover half of his face. It's just too bad they don't cover his mouth. He spits when he talks, so you have to stand there with these tiny globs of Old-Man-Stoltz spit on your face because you don't want to embarrass him by wiping it away.

He's always mad at any kid who goes near his house, and especially if someone goes on his lawn, even if it is just to chase a ball that someone kicked too hard on accident. He's always cussing up a blue streak at us "troublemakers." "You BLANK kids stay off of my BLANKING lawn or I will call every one of your BLAN-KETY-BLANKING mothers and pull your BLANKETY-BLANK ears off of every one of your stupid BLANKETY-BLANK heads!"

He uses so many words that I would have to eat an entire bar of Ivory soap for even using one if my mom heard that.

The other kids and I, we just start laughing when he goes off, and sometimes we egg Old Man Stoltz on because when he is cussing and spitting his face gets so red he looks like a giant beet that's about to explode.

"What did you say, Mr. Stoltz? I couldn't understand you!?" I would call from my bike.

"Yeah, c-c-could you p-please r-r-repeat what you s-said?" Andy would call out.

This wasn't the most respectful thing a kid can do, but then cussing in front of kids isn't too respectful either.

Mr. Stolz gets mad over the most ridiculous things, too. You should hear the sounds coming out of his house when we ring-and-run* his house. Oh my gosh, it is like nothing you have ever imagined a person could say.

One morning, my friends Andy and Tony and I were riding down the hill past Old Man Stoltz's house on our bikes. He was out

*a ring-and-run is where you sneak up to your victim's house, ring their doorbell and tear off to a hiding place where you can watch them answer the door. It gets really funny after you do it about three times, because you can always see them hiding behind their curtain watching and waiting and just when they give up you sneak up there and do it again.

in his front yard watering his grass with a hose as we sped by with playing cards in our spokes.

"WHAT THE H-E-DOUBLE-TOOTHPICKS IS ALL THAT RACKET?" he screamed.

"Hello Mr. Stoltz, how are you today?" I said in my best sing-song-y voice, slowing down enough to ride in circles on the road in front of his driveway, with Andy and Tony following me in my figure eights.

"WHAT THE BLANKETY-BLANK IS ALL THAT RACK-ET?" he shouted again, loud enough for anyone within a ten-mile radius to hear.

I screamed over the noise, "OH, WE JUST PUT SOME CARDS IN OUR SPOKES TO MAKE OUR BIKES SOUND REALLY COOL!"

"WHAT? I CAN'T HEAR YOU OVER THE BLANKETY-BLANK RACKET YOU'RE MAKING!" Then he aimed his hose at us to spray us, which made us start screaming so loud that he covered his ears and had the most annoyed look on his face.

When he went to cover his ears, that hose stuck straight up in the air, and water came down on the top of his head, totally soaking him. I laughed so hard I fell off my bike, and then Tony and Andy both piled up right on top of me, while Old Man Stoltz was so angry about getting soaked that he just let out a stream of words so blue we all covered our ears. "YOU STUPID BLANKETY-BLANK KIDS AND YOUR BLANKETY-BLANK BIKES AND YOUR BLANKETY-BLANK MOUTHS, YOU OUGHTA...."

Mrs. Stoltz stepped out on to the front porch and started screaming at the top of her lungs at him, but he couldn't hear her over his own loud shouting.

The whole thing looked like a scene out of a movie. All of

a sudden Andy rolled on his back, laughing at something inside his head that he was trying to get out, "Th-th-that g-g-gives a...."

He was laughing and snorting so hard he made Tony and me laugh even harder, and he couldn't get his whole thought out.

"That g-g-gives a whole n-n-new...." He lost it again, and now his body was convulsing so hard from his laughter that he couldn't breathe, and he started making these really weird animal noises and rolling around like he was having some kind of an attack. And then he snorted really loud, and Tony and I were just dying.

Mrs. Stoltz was looking at us, a tangled mess of bikes and boys in the street, and she kept screaming at the top of her lungs from the porch at Old Man Stoltz, who now had turned the hose her way to shut her up. He was still cursing so loud neighbors were coming out on their porches, and he was drenched like a wet dog, with his hair that he usually combs over the entire top of his head hanging in his face like an old curtain, which got me going even more when finally Andy spurted out, "It g-g-gives a whole new m-m-meaning to SP-SPITTING M-M-MAD!" This sent us all into orbit,

since we always imitate how both Old Man and Mrs. Stoltz spit when they talk. We were all rolling around in a heap, laughing so hard I almost peed my pants. I think Andy and Tony did.

My dad told me about cussing and blue streaks last summer, when my Uncle Morris was visiting us from New York, because my uncle cussed about almost everything the whole time he was with us. My mom said Uncle Morris uses the bad words as often as good decent people use normal, non-cussing words. My dad said that she should be nicer about Uncle Morris.

Dad seemed kind of mad when he talks to her about Uncle Morris: "He's had a hard life, and his only real fault is that on occasion he cusses up a blue streak."

Of course I had to find out what blue streaks had to do with cussing, since I am the curious type, and I wondered if you could actually see a blue streak when Uncle Morris cussed, just like you can see your breath on a cold, winter day.

The first morning Uncle Morris visited us last summer, we sat at breakfast as he grumbled, "Pass the BLAN-KETY-BLANK sugar for my BLANKETY-BLANK coffee! Tastes like BLAN-KETY-BLANK without it."

Uncle Morris glanced over at Carl and me then; we were staring at him. All of a sudden both Carl and I started laughing. Carl laughed so hard that milk blew out of his nose, which just made me laugh even harder. I also was looking for signs of a blue streak coming out of Uncle Morris's mouth.

"What in the BLANKETY-BLANK are you lookin' at, boy?" he growled at me.

"What's that, Uncle Morris?" I asked, knowing that when he had to repeat himself he got even more flowery with his speech.

"I *SAID*, PASS THE BLANKING..."

Mom whispered something in Dad's ear. Dad whispered something in Uncle Morris's ear, and my brother Carl and I tried really hard not to laugh out loud again, kicking each other under the table. We had both already heard some of the words Uncle Morris used from some of the teenagers down by the lake. Greg Hodapp liked to use the same kind of language - he has three older brothers who teach him all kinds of bad stuff - but Greg didn't seem to use it in the right places like Uncle Morris.

Uncle Morris always tries to act mean and tough, but we know he really likes us.

Anyway, what I wanted to say is that I was supposed to be writing in a diary all summer, but I just started on August 14th, only two weeks before I went back to school. Sister Mary Claire sent home a note to parents telling them that all the kids should keep a diary every day in the summer. No one gets to look at your diary anyhow, so I am just going to say I did it all summer, and then tell Father Cavenaugh, who is a Monsignor (the title of various senior Roman Catholic positions - basically the other priest's boss.), on Saturday in confession (which if you aren't Catholic means a formal admission of one's sins with repentance and desire of absolution,

*(p.s. I asked dad about footnotes, and he told me to add the *(asterisk) telling whoever reads this that the * means I have more to say on the subject, but it would take too much space up there, so you put it at the bottom of the page. Dad is always the English Professor.)*

esp. privately to a priest as a religious duty) that I told a lie. In case you didn't know it, priests, even Monsignors, have to take confessions to the grave with them without ever telling. They swear on a million Bibles that they will never tell all the junk they hear to another soul.

I wonder how they do that. I bet they hear really cool stuff every day that they want to tell all the other priests but can't. So, no one but him and me will know that I wasn't doing the diary every day and because I am now just using the diary as reference to remember the details, I am not going to mention it again... for awhile anyway.

CHAPTER TWO

Horacious?

My big brother Carl-io Farthead-io got me in a lot of trouble when he told on me for not feeding the cat and dogs like I am supposed to, so Mom came up to my room and made me do my chores and she wasn't very happy with me.

"Gabriel, you know the rules. You are to be responsible for the animals."

"I know, Mom."

"How would you like it if I forgot to feed you?"

"Gosh Mom, it was only one time. I was busy and..."

"You should never be too busy for your pets. They depend on you, Gabe!" Wow, Mom was really rubbing it in. I felt terrible about it, but she was making it into a real federal case. I knew I was in the wrong, but all I could think about was getting Carl back for telling on me.

Right after dinner Andy and Tyler came over and wanted to go fishing, and then after that we played hide-n-seek until Tyler's mom called him in. I headed up to my house, and as I was getting nearer, I noticed the light was blaring in our garage. It was my dad and his brother.

"Hey, Dad!"

"Hey buddy, how's things?"

"Good. How you doing, Uncle M?"

Uncle Morris just sneered at me, looked past me and then winked. That's just the way he is; he doesn't mean anything by it.

Dad and Uncle Morris were out in the garage looking under the hood of Dad's truck, getting ready to go on our trip to Yellowstone National Park. I joined in and listened to my dad and his brother talk, wondering if Carl and I would ever do stuff like this when we were grown ups.

Uncle Morris was changing the oil when he banged his head on the hood of the truck. He looked at my dad after he said, "That stupid BLANKETY-BLANKING truck is such a piece of BLANKETY-BLANK BLANKETY-BLANK. I have a BLANKETY-BLANKING lump on my BLANKETY-BLANK head the size of a BLANKETY-BLANKING ostrich egg!"

I started to giggle, imagining my Uncle with a giant egg-sized bump on his head.

"What you laughing at, kid?" Uncle Morris sneered.

I had never heard anyone actually say all of those words together at one time, and some of them I had never heard before at all, but I just knew they were really bad words by the horrified look on Mom's face when she's around them. My dad looked at my uncle with a look-that-kills kind of look he gives me if I sass him or Mom, and then he and Uncle Morris both started laughing really hard.

It was just a really good thing my mom wasn't anywhere around. She might have washed Uncle Morris's mouth out like she did my brother Carl for saying one of those words once. Uncle Morris's language really bugged my mom because she always had to put her hands on my ears so we wouldn't hear his "filthy mouth".

Well, back to Old Man Stoltz, and then back to the real bully in this story, Sister Mary Claire. Mom always says I get off the subject, but then she says that's what makes my stories interesting.

I don't even know what cussing a blue streak really means, and why blue streaks have to do with bad words, but that's what Old Man Stoltz does sometimes. He's always saying words or names, mostly God's that we use in church, but he's all angry about it, like: "JESUS H. CHRIST, YOU BLANKETY-BLANK KIDS GET OFF OF MY LAWN!"

That wasn't the first time I had heard someone saying Jesus H. I never even thought of Jesus having a middle name, but I guess he must have. I mean, it only makes sense, right? Because all moms need to call their kids by first, middle and last name when they're really angry about something. I wondered what the H. stood for. Maybe Herbert, Harry or Hal? Jesus Harry Christ, that just sounds too weird; Jesus Herbert Christ? Back then it was probably some long, boring name like Horacious: "Jesus Horacious Christ, you need to take out the garbage!"

Somehow I think Jesus must have been Mary's favorite, and she made his brothers take out the trash and do that kind of stuff while Jesus practiced walking on water and healing his cat of a bad head cold or something while he was getting ready to save the whole world, like I learn in church every morning before school starts.

I'll bet you anything when the kids aren't around, Sister Mary Claire stands in the classroom and cusses a blue streak at the black-board, where someone has written something like, "Sister Mary Claire wears old, holy*, black underwear." Or, "Sister Mary Claire, about kids she don't care. She's ugly and mean, the worst teacher I've ever seen, and under her black wimple**, she is bald without any hair!"

I think some of the Batwomen*** have to go to confession like three hundred times a day or something like that, and I bet the priests get really tired of hearing about all of their cussing and confessions of their bad attitude towards nice kids like me. But I bet none of the Batwomen ever uses the bad cusses that say things about God and His son, Jesus H. - for Horacious - Christ. THEY WOULDN'T DARE! Besides they have to respect their husband, J. C., because of the fact that He's in charge of Christmas and is the leader of the world and stuff. (I heard they are all married to him. Why would he want so many wives? And why not a pretty lady like my mom, instead of some old meanie Batwoman like Sister Mary Claire? I'll tell you what, if I had a Sister, I would hope she was

nicer that her, but then again that is a different kind of sister.)

If Sister Mary Claire wasn't such a super mean nun, I would ask her questions about this stuff, like you are supposed to be able to do with a teacher. I mean, aren't teachers there to teach you things besides just arithmetic, English and spelling junk? I wonder how many Hail Marys and Our Father Who Art in Heavens I would have to say if I tried using some of that cussing on my brother. I know we aren't supposed to use God's name bad or anything, but Old Man Stoltz is always yelling for God to do things only beavers are supposed to build.

I always imagine a big beaver dam in his front yard every time he says that word, which is like a million times a day. See, God just drops this beaver dam the size of the Empire State Building there because Old Man Stoltz asked him to.

Anyways, I just try to stay away from Old Man Stoltz as much

(Get it? Holy, meaning with holes and religious holy?) **wimple - a cloth headdress covering the head, neck, and the sides of the face, worn by nuns.* * * *(We secretly call the nuns The Batwomen. When they walk down the hall they have huge batwing hats called wimples and long flowing dresses that make them look like huge, ugly bats.)

as I can, which isn't always easy for me since his wife Mrs. Gertrude (a spitter too) Stoltz is my piano teacher and everything. How do two spitters end up getting married, anyway? Do they have spitter clubs? Geez, one time I stood in front of their house for half an hour before I would go in for my piano lesson, just to make sure Old Man Stoltz wasn't anywhere around. When I saw his car pull out of the driveway and turn at the end of the road I knocked on the door. Mrs. Stoltz wasn't too happy with me for being so late, and I certainly couldn't tell her it was because of her husband being a big meanie and having a bad mouth.

And, speaking of Christmas, last year Mr. and Mrs. Stoltz sent us a Christmas card, which is kind of weird since they live right down the street, so the letter had to go to the North Pole and all, and then back to Venus Avenue, instead of them just walking like a block and dropping it into our mailbox. My brother told me Christmas cards have to go through the North Pole to get to people because of the special Christmas stamps people use. Well anyway, that Christmas card they sent us had this dopey picture in it of Mr. and Mrs. Stoltz all dressed up like "Santa Claus and his Missus," as my dad would say. I know the guy that comes to our door every Christmas Eve in the fake Santa suit is Old Man Stoltz because his beard is all spit-y, not really but that would be funny. I always act like the candy cane he gives me is the greatest thing so he will put in a good word for me with the real Santa.

Truthfully, lately I

have been wondering about the whole Santa and the North Pole thing anyway. The weirdest thing is Old Man Stoltz doesn't even like kids at all, so why he pretends to be Santa is a mystery. That's probably just one of those things you do because your wife tells you to.

One of these days Old Man Stoltz is going to ask God to do that thing that beavers build when he is all dressed in red, and that is going to be a hoot. I'll tell you what, that is going to be worth watching - kind of like that time the lunchtime television clown Bunky the Clown cussed a kid out for pulling off his big red nose right on the show, where kids could hear him. I mean, can you imagine what that poor kid must have thought, being cussed out by a clown? I would have loved to be there to see that one, but I am deathly afraid of clowns so that won't happen.

Oops, I did it again. I wandered way far away from my subject. Now back to Sister Mary Dumbhead Batwoman Claire, the world's meanest nun of all time. I can see it on Sister Mary Claire's face when she looks at me. She tries to act all calm and all, but I can tell she always wants to ring my neck. I just nod and say, "I'm so sorry, Sister Mary Claire." But I never really even understood what I'd done to make her so mad at me. I'm glad she isn't a spitter, because she moves her face in real close to you when she chews you out, and usually her breath smells like nasty broccoli. Imagine if she started spitting broccoli at people, YUCK!

Fall is coming and winter snows will be here soon! Man oh man; I have to go weed the garden for my dad. I am going to write later today in my secret hideout - the tree house across the street where no one can find me.

I think today is the day for me to get my next detective of the month book. *The Happy Hollisters* series is my favorite. I have about eighty of those books. The Happy Hollisters are a family that goes around getting into trouble all the time and solving mysteries. But Pete is the oldest boy, and he is pretty cool the way he handles the bully, a mean guy named Joey, who is like my even meaner brother, who always thinks he can push people around.

I wish I were Pete. I would love to be in the Hollister family, but I wouldn't ever tell my mom or dad that cause they would feel bad. I mean, I like our family and all, but nothing great ever happens around here. There are no real mystery stories to solve or anything. I mean, the Happy Hollisters get into some trouble everywhere they go, and the author of the books had to get the ideas for that somehow.

My brother always makes fun of my books; he thinks 'the happy' anything sounds dorky. He says no one can always be happy, but the Happy Hollisters are always happy. I think he is just jealous. I think someday I am going to be a super spy, and when I retire from that I will write books like Jerry West, who writes the *The Happy Hollisters*. I bet he was a spy or something like that in Russia before he started writing about the Hollisters, and that's where he got all the cool ideas for the stuff they do.

So I am going to move to Russia and be a secret detective spy code named Dirk The Smirk, and then I will have a lot to write about when I am old like my dad.

By the way, the other day I was at Eddie's house watching this really cool black-and-white show on television about this sheriff in a place called Mayberry when this other show came on called *The Flying Nun*. It was so fake. I mean, there is this nun who looks like someone's big sister and she is always smiling. I have never seen a nun who looks like anything that isn't pruney and wrinkled, and there are almost no nuns who smile. Matter of fact, the only one I can think of is Sister Anne Martin. She is nice, but that is it!

Maybe I will be a sheriff when I grow up. I could be a sheriff and a spy. That would be my cover, like a super-secret spy no one suspects, cause I go around giving people tickets for parking in the wrong place, but I am actually watching a Russian spy who is pretending to be the dense barber but is really a double-crossing double agent.

CHAPTER THREE

The Batwomen

Weirdo Mrs. Abernathy and her two fluffy-headed twins took me to school this morning. The first day, and it was their turn instead of Mom's to drive, just my luck. I have a feeling it is going to be the best part about my day, and it wasn't good. School is back in session, OH YEA!

All the nuns in my school are crabby, 'cept for Sister Anne Martin, who is the assistant to Mother Superior. So to explain it to people who don't go to parochial school, the Mother Superior is like a principal, and the assistant is like the Assistant Principal. Sister Anne Martin can't bring herself to swat or smack us kids like all the other nuns, who seem to kind of like doing it with their long rulers.*

So, when a kid gets in trouble and Sister Ann Martin is in charge, instead of him getting beat up on, she closes the door and then she slaps the desk hard for every stroke she is supposed to be giving him, and then she blows a little pepper in his eyes right

---

* When I get big I am going to outlaw wood rulers and invent real soft rubber rulers, so all the kids who get smacked by them can just act like it hurts and then the joke will be on God's wife.

before he leaves her office to make them water like he is really crying. Notice how I said "he:" GIRLS NEVER GET IN TROUBLE! They can do the exact same thing a boy does, and they don't get sent to see Mother Superior.

It's kind of funny because Mrs. Ward, the school secretary, always gives the person in trouble a piece of candy when they come out from one of Sister Anne Martin's "swattings" cause she feels sorry for them, so not only don't they get spanked for being bad, but they get candy as well.

Sometimes I'm tempted to get in trouble just to get a free piece of candy, but one time this kid named Freddy did that, and he ended up getting his punishment from Mother Superior, who was supposed to be on vacation but stayed because she had something called shingles, which made her ultra-grumpy and probably spank harder than normal. Mother Superior is the pitcher for the Batwomen's softball team, and has one mean paddle because of her backswing. Freddy Goodnight couldn't sit down for a week after Mother Superior smacked him. Mother Superior and Sister Mary Claire are the two meanest ladies I have ever met, well except for Mean Mrs. Rickles (more on her later... oooohhh haahaa).

The Batwomen's softball team is actually called the Catholic Lady's Bingo Bombers (or CLBB, said like 'club,' get it?), with nuns* and some big, fat moms, except for this one mom who is like ten feet tall and weighs as much as I do. She is a star shortstop, which cracks me up that she is called a 'shortstop,' since she is the tallest, skinniest human being I have ever seen.

It is so funny to watch the nuns playing softball in those big dresses. They do wear these funny habits that don't have the stiff batwing stuff so that when they are running they don't fly away, which is what I pray happens to Sister Mary Claire every night. Sister Mary Claire plays second base, and I swear I have seen her stick her foot out to trip a mom or a nun from the other team who is trying to steal base. She wears these black shoes with white socks pulled way up on her leg and it looks totally dorky. I wonder if a nun has to go to confession for stealing a base, since it is one of the Ten Commandments, 'Thou Shalt Not Steal...?'

Some of the older kids at school have told us younger kids that Sister Anne Martin was doing that fake paddling stuff way back when they were little like us, but no one ever tells. No one really wants to get hit, so we all keep her secret. If only every Sister in the school were like Sister Anne Martin!

Speaking of getting in trouble at school, one time I got

* A Nun is the same as a Sister, it's capitalized because it's a title, not like your little sister, which is not. A nun is also the name of some pigeon, which looks like a Sister or a Batwoman, except for Sister Anne Martin, who seems too nice to be a Nun and would be a nice sister, but then you would have to call her Sister sister Anne Martin, who is a nun, by the way.

caught drinking holy water on the back steps of the church, which I did for only good reasons, figuring that if a little on your forehead makes you a better Catholic, a better person, then drinking it would make your whole soul better, inside and out clean, like Mr. Clean on T.V. with the pirate earring and the bald head like my friend Eddie's dad (not the earring part). But I got caught by one of the priests during morning prayer time, and he marched me over to Mother Superior's office for a good swatting, but because Mother Superior was busy with other business they sent me to Sister Anne Martin's office instead, and she did that whole slap-the-desk thing with me. I put on a great show; every time she slapped down on the desk, I moaned and groaned so loud that everyone on the whole ten-acre St. Joseph's property could hear me.

Sister Anne Martin whispered for me to calm down, that I was really overdoing it. So I just cried out every so often as the ruler came down on the desk. I was laughing so hard I thought I would split my sides.

Sister Anne Martin started laughing too, and suddenly she started to snort, which cracked us both up so bad it brought tears to her eyes and mine. When I left her office, the tears were still streaming down my cheeks, and Mrs. Ward looked at me with the saddest eyes I have ever seen. She got up from her desk where she was pounding away on a typewriter, probably trying to drown out the sound of my yelling and screaming, and gave me a big hug. It was weird; she smelled just like cotton candy. I didn't know people could smell like cotton candy.

Mrs. Ward handed me a Black Cow, which is like the totally best candy in the world, and I almost went right back to the church to drink more holy water, hoping I would get caught and get sent back to Sister Anne Martin and get another Black Cow. But if it happened twice in one day, they would probably call my mom, and not that she would think what I did was so bad or anything, but it would be a problem for her and I didn't want to do that.

There is only one teacher at school who isn't married to Jesus. Her name is Mrs. Sampson. She's married to Mr. Sampson, this funny-looking guy with hair growing right on top of his nose. He always has gray coveralls on all the time and lots of grease down his front from fixing Volkswagen cars. When it is nice weather Mrs. Sampson eats lunch with him every day on the front lawn, where we are not allowed to go during the school day without a teacher. But we can see her from the windows, and one time I even saw Mr. Sampson lean over and kiss her on the cheek, ohhh-la-la my friends would say (Andy would probably say ohhhh-l-l-la-l-la). They sit on a blanket and eat lunch, just like they are having a picnic every day, instead of just a few times in the summer like my family does when we drive up into the mountains. Mrs. Sampson told me Mr. Sampson owns a garage just one block from the school, and he walks over to meet her every day for lunch.

I think that it would be a nice thing if all moms and dads had picnics every day together. I think I will do that when I am a grownup.

Mrs. Sampson is short and has hair the color of my burgundy blazer that I only wear on Fridays when we have special communion. She is the nicest lady I have ever, ever met, except for maybe my grandma and my mom. All the kids like Mrs. Sampson, and it isn't only because she isn't a mean old nun. She really likes kids, and I think she is a grandma too, so she understands why we do what we do.

I had her in first grade as a teacher. I wish she taught every grade, because Sister Mary Claire is the absolute worst person to ever put on the Batwoman costume, and she totally, totally, totally HATES ME!

CHAPTER FOUR

Movie Star Gabe

During the first two months of my second fourth-grade year, the strangest thing happened. Because my school goes from kindergarten to twelfth grade, there are a lot of kids in all shapes and sizes. There is this group of guys who remind me of what my friends and me will be when the Secret Detective Brotherhood Club grows up. Anyway, their leader, this tall guy named Donny Jones, was walking past me in the hall, and then stepped right in front of me and said, "Hey guys, look at this kid."

Uh oh, I thought. It's bad enough when kids my age make fun of me for being a geek, but now this? I was frozen in place, just waiting to see what they were going to do to me, praying that one of the Sisters would come down the hall quickly before I ended up in the bathroom getting a swirly from the biggest guys in the school.

"Who does this kid remind you of?" Donny Jones grunted again.

"Heck, I don't know," the kid with red hair and freckles, who looks like Andy, said. "Who?"

Oh man, I thought, he said heck. That is so close to H-E-

Double-Toothpicks that if one of the Sisters heard him he would get it good. I wondered if twelfth graders still got the ruler or if they got some other penance since they're bigger than most of the nuns and all.

"Come on, he's a dead ringer. Think!"

"Your kid sister?" Another kid in their group laughed.

OUCH! Nice, I thought, Now I look like someone's sister.

"No, you idiot - Eddie."

"Who?" we all said at once.

"Eddie, on The Courtship of Eddie's Father*. Dude, he looks exactly like Eddie!"

"HOLY COW, YOU'RE RIGHT!" the red-haired kid shouted.

"Our own little movie star right here at good old Saint Joe's!" Donny Jones announced, and hoisted me up on his shoulder. He carried me down the hall and lifted me off in front of a group of the most popular girls in the whole school.

*The Courtship of Eddie's Father was a popular television show in the late 60s and early 70s

31

"Who does this kid look like to you?"

"Huh?" Tina Anders, leader of the St. Joe's Cheerleaders, sighed.

"Come on Tina, think, who does this kid look just like?"

Tina looked at me with total boredom. "My kid brother?"

"No, think of movie stars." he grunted.

The other boys looked on with smug looks of knowing.

"Duh, Donnie, I don't know. Why you buggin' this poor little kid?" She twirled her gum around her finger while it was still in her mouth. It was totally illegal to chew gum at St. Joe's, but she was twirling hers without worrying about any of the Sisters who might be walking up and down the hall seeing her.

"E D D I E on The Courtship of Eddie's Father! Check it out, it's him!"

"Oh my gosh, he is sooooo cute! He does look just like him. Oh my gosh, it's little Eddie!" Tina Anderson gave me this big hug.

And then all of the cheerleaders gathered around me, talking about how cute I was, like I was some kind of a zoo animal or puppy. I couldn't believe it. I didn't make the connection, but when I got home, there was this Tiger Beat magazine on my desk that I had found near my brother's bus stop. I flipped through it looking for the kid that played Eddie, and when I found a little picture of him with Bill Bixby, his dad on the show, I couldn't believe the resemblance. It was kind of like looking at a better-looking twin.

Later, as the family sat down at dinner, I announced that they could start calling me Eddie. I told them the whole story, and showed them the picture in the magazine.

Things were really going to change for me at school now. In one day, I had been transformed from "Peters the repeater" to the mascot for the twelfth-grade cheerleading squad, and the coolest boys in the school would want me to hang around with them.

As I climbed up the stairs to go to my room, Carl busted by me, pushing me back downstairs with his big hand on my head. "Move aside, MOVIE STAR LOSER!"

He dashed to his room and slammed his door shut. I could hear him laughing in there, and I thought of a million and one ways that I was going to get back at him.

So, I guess all the talk about me being just like that kid on t.v. was going to my head, because I went into the second-floor bathroom and started acting like a famous singer with my hairbrush in front of the mirror. All of a sudden, there is noise outside the bathroom window. I looked over, thinking it might be a big bird or something, but there was my ugly brother Carl's mug pushed up against the window, greasing it up and everything with his nose. And his friend Greg was staring at me and laughing so hard at me that he fell off the ladder and landed on top of Mom's rhubarb plant, totally squishing it, which Carl blamed on me later.

I have never been so embarrassed in all my life. I mean, come on, the door is locked for privacy, and those goons sneak up the ladder to watch me being a super rock 'n roller. I am planning on getting back at them, no doubt about that. ONE RED ANT SURPRISE COMING UP!

Lately my buddies, the members of the Secret Detective Brotherhood, and me have been talking about how sick and tired we are of our older brothers making fun of us and picking on us all the time. I decided this is the straw that is going to break the camel's back. I am going to call a special, secret meeting to see what the other guys want to do to get the older jerks back. LIKE I SAID, ONE RED ANT SURPRISE COMING UP!

CHAPTER FIVE

New Kid

Andy came down to my house early this morning. I was sound asleep in my tent. He whispered, "G-G-Gabe, you al-lone?"

"Yeah," I answered.

Butch was going to spend the night, but he had to go to some family thing early so he couldn't. Andy pushed in next to me, and was lying on his back looking at the roof of the tent, but not saying much. He looked really bad, like something big was bothering him. His eyes were really red and his face was too. The last time I saw him this upset was when he stuck stickers all over his dad's car and got in a ton of trouble. I always know when he wants to talk.

"Hey, you wanna go up to my room?"

"Wh-whatever." Andy sounded real sad.

We left to go sit in my room, but not saying much. I was petting Flop, and he was purring so loud it sounded like the lawn mower. Andy was picking stuff up, but looking right through it. He wasn't really interested in anything, just filling the time. All of sudden he started to talk.

"My d-d-dad came in r-r-really l-late last night and he had b-been at a b-bar again..."

"Mmmm."

I never know what to say when Andy talks about his dad. Usually Andy doesn't stutter very much when it is just us, but he was pretty upset.

"As usual I c-c-can't sleep when they argue, so I was j-j-just lying there w-wondering w-what w-was going on d-down there. All four of m-my brothers came out into the hall whispering about wh-what they should d-d-do. Dad and mom started y-yelling, th-then I heard a loud crash. J-Johnny ran down the stairs and grabbed D-dad's arm. He was g-going to throw this v-vase at my m-mom."

All of a sudden Andy started crying really hard.

"He left and d-didn't come back until this m-m-morning."

"Man, I'm so sorry you have to put up with all that stuff."

I just didn't really ever know what to say. I felt so bad for my best friend, but I just couldn't understand how anyone's dad could do the stuff Andy's dad did. I was afraid of Andy's dad, and I couldn't imagine what it would be like to live with him.

"M-m-mom came up and t-told us to go back to bed and not to w-worry too much about my d-dad. She was t-telling us that he was just h-having a hard time and w-would change soon, but M-Mom's been saying that for a l-l-long time. Johnny came and got m-me, and we all slept in the same room on the floor. It was w-weird... Johnny and Jeremy are b-b-bigger than my dad, but they act really scared of him s-sometimes. I think my d-dad is g-g-going insane. After Dad left, Jeremy went downstairs and took all of the b-b-ottles out of the liquor cabinet and p-poured them all down the s-sink."

"Oh man, your dad must be steamed!"

"That's the w-weird thing. When my d-dad came into the kitchen this m-m-morning, he saw the empty b-bottles sitting in the sink where Jeremy had l-left them, and just mumbled something under his b-breath. He then just s-s-sat on the back p-p-patio for a long time staring. M-my mom was t-t-talking to my Uncle Rich about it, and it sounded l-l-like they are going to try to get my d-dad into some hospital for drinkers."

"Wow, Andy, that stinks..."

"B-b-big time."

Andy just sat there for a long time sniffling. I could tell he was crying, but I never looked up so he wouldn't be embarrassed.

I wish he could come live with us. I am so afraid that his mom is going to move his family away like Tyler's did.

Mom knew something was going on because she invited Andy to eat breakfast with us, and then later to eat lunch with us. I guess it was so he wouldn't have to go home. Dad was golfing with his buddies and having a special birthday lunch at his favorite restaurant, which gave Mom time to plan the party. I knew she was talking to Andy's mom on the phone, but he didn't know that.

"Boys, I am going shopping for Dad's birthday dinner. Andy, you are welcome to come for dinner if you would like."

"Thanks, Mrs. P-P-Peters, but I'm not too sure Mr. P-Peters would l-like me being there at his birthday p-party."

Mom put her arm around Andy's shoulder. "Andy, you're like a member of this family. If it's okay with your mom, then it's okay with us."

Andy called his mom. He didn't say much, lots of uh huhs and hmmms, but I could tell the answer was no about dinner. "Mrs. Peters, M-M-Mom said I n-needed to come home for supper, but wanted me to thank you for having me over."

"Young man, you're welcome anytime you want to be here."

Andy smiled really big.

"Mom, can we sleep out in the tent tonight?"

"Well, we'll see what your father has planned."

Andy looked over at me, and I knew just by the look on his face that he was ready to go out and have some fun and try to forget about all of his troubles at home. Best friends can tell when their friend needs to talk and when they need to do something to just forget about the things they were talking about. We needed to go have some new adventures, and we needed to go explore more to find out more of what the new kid who had just moved into the neighborhood was all about. We knew he was about our age, but now we were going to find out if he was the kind of kid we would want in the Secret Brotherhood.

Keith Murphy had moved into the neighborhood a couple of weeks before summer ended, and according to the other guys who rode the bus with him, he was just as obnoxious at school as he was at home. They all played rock, paper, scissors to decide who was going to have to ride next to him in the school bus. Keith Murphy claims to be the world's greatest authority on World War II* - and every other war for that matter - and that is all he wants to talk about, according to the other guys.

* World War II - a war (1939-45) in which the Axis Powers (Germany, Italy and Japan) were defeated by an alliance including the U K and its dominions, the Soviet Union and the U.S. Hitler's invasion of Poland in September 1939 led Great Britain and France to declare war on Germany. Germany defeated and occupied France in 1940, and soon overran much of Europe. Italy joined the war in 1940, and the U.S. and Japan entered after the Japanese attacked Pearl Harbor. Italy surrendered in 1943, and the Allies launched a invasion in Normandy, France, in June 1944. The war in Europe ended when Germany surrendered in May 1945; Japan surrendered after the U.S. dropped atom bombs on Hiroshima and Nagasaki in August 1945.

He seems like a pretty okay guy to me. A little weird, but it's hard when you are the new kid, trying to join in with a bunch of guys who have known each other basically their whole lives. The first time I met him, he started talking about war and all these battles that took place over in Europe. He talks so fast it is hard to interrupt him or tell him you don't want to hear any more: "Sowhenthealliedforcesmoved intothecities...Therewere bunkerswheretheGermanswere...OnetimetheJapanesewerecombing thisislandforlandminesand...SowereallysockedittothematNormandy ...MyGrandpatoldmethatifwehadn't...Iwasonetimereadthisthingabo utChurchill,hewasgoingto..."

Some of his stories sounded a lot like the stories Mr. Povich used to tell me when I went up to his house to mow his lawn.

Anyway, Keith Murphy always wants to play war or talk about war. It is the only thing he is interested in, and no matter what we are doing he turns it into some kind of a war game. Like when we play car light duck, and he is It (which means he has to be the one to stand in the yard by the big curve in the road and get hit by car lights and do something wild to get the driver's attention and then run and hide), he sneaks up on you and acts like he threw a grenade in your trench or other hidey-hole. But he throws sticks and stuff, which doesn't feel too good. Then when you complain, he starts talking a mile a minute and you can't work a word in, "Oh,you'rejustluckyIdidn'tbringmyWorldWarTworeplicas.Weuse dthoseinourwarsinmyoldneighborhood.Everyonehereistoosissy!"

It gets kind of old really quick.

Keith Murphy tries too hard sometimes to try to fit in, like when he showed up at the streetlight for hide-n-seek dressed up all in camouflage and with some of his mom's mascara on his cheeks to darken his face because he thinks he is a World War Two expert. "HeydidyouguysknowthatinNormandytherewerethese..."

"Stop it with war all the time Murphy, jeez..." Carl barked.

"Yeah, give us a break! Who cares about that old stuff anyhow?" Carl's best friend Greg snapped, standing shoulder to shoulder with Carl.

Murph just stood there with his mouth hanging open. No one said another word, so he just walked away. I felt bad hearing him say under his breath in a growl, "It's Murph, not Murphy, that's what all my friends used to call me." I could see that he was going home, and the way his shoulders were slumping I could tell he was sad and felt lonely.

Murphy is a War Boy. That's all he talks about. I am tired of all his garbage! SHUT YOUR MOUTH! I want to shout! I want to make him sit on a red ant pile and watch them climb in his pants Because then he'll have ants in his shorts and that will make him dance.

"That guy is so annoying, " Butch scowled. Butch is the one who hassles Murph the most. For some reason it doesn't seem like Murph and Butch will ever get along. "I wish he hadn't moved here!"

"How can we ditch him?" Greg snapped, looking at my friends and me like we were the reason Murph had moved to our neighborhood in the first place.

I felt bad for Murph. He was just trying to make friends. I wasn't too interested in what he had to say either, but I know how it feels to be left out all the time.

The next morning I was getting ready to go fishing and was about to call Andy to see if he could go when Murph called me and asked me what I was doing. Mom overheard me talking and figured out that it was Murph, "Ask him to go with you too, Gabe. A new kid needs friends."

The whole time we were fishing, Murph kept throwing rocks into water below Tunnel Number One, acting every time like he was pulling a pin and dropping a grenade on the enemy in a sub: "Look,thereedsaremoving!Theyaresneakingunderthe bridgeto-blowitup...Thetrainwillspilloverthecliffifwedon'tstop them!"

Murph was yelling so loud there wasn't a fish for a mile that would ever bite one of our worms as long as he was there. There is no way a fish will bite when someone is showering them with rocks. "Keith, stop throwing rocks!" I whisper-yelled.

"Notthrowingrocks,they'regrenades,andmyfriendscall meMurphPrivatePeters!" Murph sneered and threw another one right down by where my hook was dangling.

"P-Private P-P-Peters?" Andy scoffed

"SHUT UP PRIVATE EPSTEIN!" I laughed.

"Come on, M-Murph, let us f-f-fish!" Andy growled.

" W a t c h t h e f l a n k s , P r i v a t e P e t e r s . Theyarecominguptheotherside.Throwagrenade!" Murph yelled.

"Why are you acting like such a jerk? AND STOP CALL-ING ME PRIVATE PETERS!" The words came spilling out of my mouth before I could hold them back.

Murph spun around and leered at me, "Ihateithere. Everyoneissoboring.Weneverwentfishinginmyoldneighborhood.IT' S S T U P I D ! W e p l a y e d a r m y l i k e r e a l m e n . "

Murph's face was all red and ugly, like he wanted to punch me or throw me off the tunnel. He threw another rock in the water right where my line was going in.

"Geez, I am out of h-here! This g-g-guy's an idiot!" Andy scowled, reeling in his line. And then he started walking down the tracks toward tunnel number two.

"Forget it!" I agreed, and started reeling in my line.

"Wait, Peters!" Murph stood there with his mouth hanging open and the saddest look on his face.

But I had kept asking him to stop, and he didn't. I don't like fishing with Murph. As a matter of fact, I don't like Murph much. I feel bad about it, but the truth is he is really, really hard to like.

So, basically Murph says he knows everything there is to know about the battles and the enemy and always has people quiz him. He wants us to play army all the time, which is fun for a while, but we like to do other things, too.

Even though Murph was mostly aggravating, we took a vote in the Secret Brotherhood to let Murph in, because we need numbers. You know the old saying, "There's strength in numbers?" With all of our mean older brothers, it helps to have another person in our club with us. Besides, he is big for his age and brags about all these fights he has gotten into in his old school, he calls them hand-to-hand-combat-conflicts. The truth is he reminds me of the kid Ronnie who used to beat up on me at school, and I wonder if he might have been his last school's bully. But I guess that is even more reason to have him on my side, just in case.

One day we were watching our big brothers from the tree house with binoculars. They were carrying shovels and pails and bags of stuff to their "secret fort." After they were up there for a while, we snuck up the ditch and watched them from the hill above their fort. Good old Murph went with us, and of course he turned the "secret fort" into World War II bunkers, and we were all suddenly on an island out in the South Pacific hunting the enemy.

Though I didn't want to admit it to anyone else, playing war was a lot more fun than it seemed at first. If only Murph didn't have to give us all a long history lesson every time. So one by one all the guys started leaving. I could hear Butch muttering about how he just couldn't take Murph anymore.

Andy and Murph and I were the only one's left when Murph said, "Hey,guysyouwannastartOperation RedAntRevenge?" We all three started laughing at the thought of it.

"Let's d-d-do it!" Andy was excited.

I nodded too, and grabbed the coffee can I had rescued from the trash with the plastic lid, and the three of us went to the biggest red anthill we knew of down on the dirt trail where we jumped our bikes. When we got there we realized we had not brought a little shovel, and then we figured we could dig them out with the coffee can. When we started digging into the top of the anthill, the ants became instantly furious and started moving around a million miles an hour. Murph took a huge scoop right where they were coming out of a big hole by the thousands, and some of them got on his hands and arms and started biting.

"OUCH!OW!COMEON,GUYS,ALITTLEHELPHERE?"

We all started scooping the ants into the can, flicking them off our hands as fast as we could to keep them from biting, but they still did. Several ants crawled up my arm and got inside my shirt and started biting me as hard as they could. By the time we had scooped a bunch of the ants into the can, we were all shirtless and hitting each other on the back and front with the shirts to knock them off. Andy had several big red bumps already growing up on his chest, I had some on my arms and stomach, and Murph was covered with little red welts since he had done most of the digging and they had crawled all over him. All of a sudden Murph started screaming about them being down inside his pants. He was dancing around and suddenly just stripped down totally naked as he

43

started smacking his legs with his shirt.

Even though Andy and I were in pain, we were laughing so hard watching Murph smacking himself and dancing and screaming naked that spit and snot was just streaming out of our faces. Just then two girls came down the hill riding bikes and talking really loudly.

Murph hit the dirt and started to army crawl. Fortunately he had jumped behind one of the bike jumps and away from the red anthill where he could pull his clothes on.

"ThrowmemyunderwearPeters!" he whispered.

I acted like I didn't hear him. "Throw myskivvies, guys, comeon!"

Andy and I were laughing so hard I thought I was going to pee my pants.

Murph pulled his pants on and dove over the hill, grabbing his underwear, and then dove back behind the jump again. "THANKSALOT,GUYS!"

The two girls rode over the jumps, but didn't even lift their handlebars and try to get air, which was the whole point of a bike jump. But of course they were riding bikes with pink baskets strapped to the handlebars and dolls along for the ride in the baskets. They looked at us like we were from Mars, but of course I was from Venus. And then they rode and disappeared down the dirt trail while talking loudly enough for us to hear about how boys were all such weirdos.

Murph crawled out from behind the jump where he had been hiding. "Comeon,guys,let'smoveonwithOperationRedAnt Revenge!" Murph screamed, still slapping his ant bites.

All three of us moved up the dirt trail with the coffee can, scratching and slapping the spots on us where the ants had taken out their revenge.

When we got back up the tree house, Murph explained the whole Operation Red Ant Revenge mission and how it was going to work. He would lead us out and we would be his scouts when he need-ed us. He drew the whole thing on the tree house floor with his finger.

On his signal we each shimmied down the rope and dropped to the ground, follow-ing his lead. We rolled across the dirt and dropped down into the ditch and started to crawl up the ditch in the muddy water and of course, Murph kept talking about it like we were over on some Pacific island somewhere.

We crawled for quite a way, until we were just across from where the secret fort was, and waited there in the ditch for a long time. And finally Carl and his friends left their diggings and headed down toward the railroad tracks.

Murph barked in a low voice, "Petersyoutaketheleftflank, Epsteintheright!" Andy rolled his eyes, and he and I looked at each

45

other like Murph had just spoken Spanish.

"FLANK?" Andy and I said at the same time.

"Justwatchtheoppositesidesofthefortttomakesureyousig-naliftheenemyreturns!Handsignalsunlessitisacodered,thenwemove-toaudible."

"You mean yell or whistle 'Murph'?" I teased.

Murph ignored me.

Andy and I crept low to the ground, each standing behind a tree and a clump of bushes, waiting for Murph to go. We gave the okay signal with our fingers to tell Murph that no one was nearby.

When the coast was clear, Murph, who was holding the coffee can full of red ants, started crawling down the ditch real slowly. I noticed he had covered his face with mud to camouflage himself I guess. He belly-crawled all the way down the ditch on his hands and knees, which really wasn't necessary, but I guess that's how you deliver the package, as Murph called it, when you are in a war. He looked left to me - I signaled a-okay - then right to Andy, he signaled a-okay - then Murph climbed out of the ditch and army-crawled down the embankment to the secret fort where he lifted the piece of plywood they had over the top of the hole and dumped the whole can in, which must have been about a million red ants. Murph crawled back up the embankment and let out a yelp, slapping his arm, which I assumed meant a few of the ants had crawled out of the can and back on him.

Then Murph ran reallow to the ground in the opposite direction that the brothers had gone. Andy and I ran toward him and the three of us jumped the barbwire fence and headed across the farmer's cow pasture. Murph acted like he was on horseback, and kept slapping his backside like he was trying to get his horse to run faster. Andy started doing the same, and then I joined in. We were galloping through the cow pasture whooping and hollering about how funny it was going to be the next time our mean big brothers were down in their secret fort. We tied up our horses, and then crossed the highway over to the bait shop to see good old Joe and tell him about our latest prank. Joe was good at keeping secrets.

For some reason, I guess it was because Andy and I went along with the whole war scenario when dropping Operation Red Ant Revenge, Murph thought we wanted to spend the rest of the day playing army, but Andy and I had had enough. We made some excuse that we both had to go home

We ditched Murph, and after a little while a bunch of us guys were sitting under the streetlight when the mysterious Denise walked by. She was a very pretty girl; anybody could see that, and some of our older brothers seemed to have crushes on her.

"Yuck, what's so great about her?" I asked anyone who was listening, and not totally glued on Denise.

I watched Carl watching Denise. I don't know how to explain it, but it made me feel kind of jealous that my brother thought she was so great. He and his friends were always talking about her and trying to get her attention without ever really even talking to her.

"I dare you to walk her home and tell her you love her," I taunted my brother.

"Love? Chicken-little! Love her? What are you talking about, love?"

"Well, you sure look like you do." I said snidely.

My friends chimed in, "Yeah C-Carl, you ch-chicken to tell her how you really f-f-feel?"

"Shut up or I'll pound you all!" Carl snarled in a low voice, so she wouldn't hear him.

I felt the shiver move up my spine and watched it move around the circle, except for Andy. He had big brothers and wasn't scared of mine, because he knew there was no way any of the older guys would mess with him, knowing then that they would be messing with the four older Epsteins, two of them who were sitting in the circle right now

"Yeah, w-well, I say you're ch-chicken of her," Andy blurted.

I saw a dare-off coming.

Just then Murph came up and joined the group. "Sothat's whereyouguyshavebeen.Ibeentoeveryone'shouse,andnoone's-momknewwhereyouwere.Secretmission,huh?"

No one said a word to Murph.

Murph jumped in again, "Well,girlsarenobigdeal. S'matteroffact, dur- ingtheBigInvasion,thesenurseswererounoundin-gup..."

"SHUT UP, MURPHY!" everyone said in unison.

Denise turned and looked right at my brother, smiled, and disappeared around the corner where this other girl met her.

Somehow I knew the next dare off was going to be on know-it-all-Murph.

Carl stood up, stretched and said, "This is lame and it's getting a little cold. Come on, Greg, let's go see what's up on T.V."

Greg looked at him curiously. My brother nodded his head in the direction Denise had gone. Then they both walked down the street in the opposite direction of either one of their houses heading up the gravel road toward the "secret fort."

About a half hour later we saw Carl, Greg, Denise and her friend heading up the gravel road toward the "secret fort."

Andy, Murph and I looked at each other, our eyes wide. Oh, this was going to be better than we thought. I wondered if they would find the red ants we had dumped in there.

Later, I was just settling into my sleeping bag in my tent. My dog Frisky was sleeping at the back of the tent, and Friskier was outside on the grass. Andy poked his head in.

"C-can I sleep h-h-here tonight?"

"Sure! You look like you saw a ghost." I whispered.

He looked pretty bad, his eyes were wide and freaked out.

"They t-t-took m-my dad away tonight. M-My Uncle Richie came, and they got into a fight. Dad punched h-h-im right in th-the jaw, but my Uncle w-w-wouldn't hit him back, he just put him in a huge bear hug and got him into his truck. Uncle Richie t-t-told me things w-would be b-better now, b-but that Dad was g-going to be g-gone for l-like a month. I j-just couldn't t-t-take listening to my M-Mom's crying anymore, and my brothers are in a really bad mood. Can I stay here?"

Andy was sniffling a lot and I could tell he had been crying.

"Sure." I said, wanting to know the right thing to say, but sometimes it is too hard to know when there doesn't seem to be anything that could make the situation better.

Andy's sleeping bag was under his arm. He flopped down on the cot next to me and Frisky sat next to him, pushing his nose into Andy's armpit. That made Andy laugh and Frisky's tail go wild.

Within a minute Andy was snoring really loud. I wondered if maybe my parents could adopt him so he wouldn't be so sad.

The next morning I snuck out of the tent in into the house. Andy was sound asleep. He had tossed and turned all night with bad dreams, so I thought I'd just let him sleep.

I heard Carl whining and complaining in his room. I tiptoed across the hall and peeked in. Mom was sitting on his bed with him, putting this bright pink stuff all over him. He looked like he had giant pink measles, and I could see that there were a thousand little ant bites that Mom still had to treat. I wondered if at that very moment Greg and the girls were doing the very same thing. I ran back to the tent where I muffled my laughter into my pillow and then Andy and I whispered about how well the operation Murph had planned had worked out. It cheered him up a bit. By the time we both imagined what must have gone on in their secret fort with the girls we were rolling around on the ground, cracking each other up.

This was too good. I just had to tell Murph and the rest of the guys.

But even though I figured that pink stuff stopped the itching and I needed it bad from my own red ant attack, I wasn't about to tell anyone about my own bites right now.

Carl and his dumb big friend
Climbed deep into the dirts
with a big red ant surprise
Their whole body's have bite hurts!

CHAPTER SIX

Halloween

It's hard to believe I have already been in school for over two months. Time goes so much slower during the school year, and summers zip by way too fast.

I hear other kids saying in August that they are getting bored and that there is nothing to do. I am never bored. There is always something to do, and the summertime is the best time to do it. BUT, I really like Halloween, too, and Thanksgiving and Christmas and... come to think of it, it would be really cool if the whole year was vacations, holidays and summer.

They say some legends are born on cold dark nights. I believe what they, whoever they are, say is true. I know because of what happened on Halloween night this year, and if I hadn't been there to see it with my own eyes, I never would have believed it happened at all. Even now I wonder if it was all just a dream, because it just doesn't seem like it could have really happened.

But as I walked up the icy, cold path off the gravel road, right past the spooky old lady's house in my cape and fangs, I had no idea I was about to see something that could be used as blackmail on my older brother for years to come. But somehow that isn't how it turned out at all.

This girl Denise had moved in to our neighborhood last summer, and no one knew much about her. All the older boys said she was foxy, which means super cute, and followed her around everywhere. My brother acted like she was no big deal, but the rumors in the neighborhood were that Denise had a major crush on him. So, now with what I know, it is no coincidence that she dressed like a she-werewolf and my brother dressed like a he-werewolf. They were the perfect fuzzy couple.

It is funny to see a girl with hair glued to her face. It's like the bearded lady at the carnival who probably glues her beard on too. It would be totally gross if she really had a beard like a dad.

Every Halloween, there is a big party in the Anderson's barn nearby, with old-fashioned dunking for apples, and games like that.

There is this really cool show on t.v. every Friday night that Mom lets us stay up late to watch. Actually my mom loves monster movies, so she stays up really late with us sometimes, and makes a huge bowl of popcorn and lots and lots of snacks and soda pop to go along with the "Creature Features." Our favorite movies are the ones about Frankenstein*, Dracula** and the Werewolf***.

So this year for Halloween some of us decided to go as the monsters from the shows. Carl picked the Werewolf. I was going as Dracula, and Andy was going to be Frankenstein, which is the hardest costume to make if you think about it. The coolest things

*Frankenstein is a character in the novel Frankenstein by Mary Shelley. Baron Frankenstein is a scientist who creates and brings to life a man-like monster that eventually turns on him and destroys him; Frankenstein is not the name of the monster itself, as is often assumed. **Dracula is the vampire from a place called Transylvania in Bram Stoker's novel Dracula (1897). It is the name given to Vlad the Impaler, a 15th-century prince of Wallachia renowned for his cruelty. ***Werewolf is a person who changes into a wolf, typically when there is a full moon.

about Dracula, other than the fact that he lives forever and goes around sucking the blood from pretty ladies and can fly all over the place and show up on the tops of buildings to take his next victim, is his cape and fangs.

My dad, being a college professor, has to attend a lot of graduation events and other fancy things, and has this really cool black cape. He let me use it for my vampire costume, but Mom had to sew it a little to make it shorter so it wouldn't drag all over the ground and get ruined. She made it kind of like high-water pants and it looked a little goofy, but I couldn't tell her that since she was working so hard to help me be Dracula. High-water Dracula, ready for a flood... of blood, that is.

I bought this tube of vampire blood at the mall's magic shop, and these fake teeth that have fangs as long as my index finger to hang down over my lips. Mom had some weird makeup called 'foundation' that makes your face totally white, and makes you look like you could be dead. The foundation of a house is made out of concrete, and that's what this stuff looks like on your face.

The vampire blood dripping down over the white makeup, and the long fangs actually makes me look really, really scary. If it weren't for the fact that I have to wear my stupid glasses everywhere I really would have looked scary, but as usual, I just looked like a nerd wannabe trying to be scary. Real vampires don't have to wear glasses.

I came out of the bathroom totally dressed up, and Frisky and Friskier were sitting in the hall waiting for me. I think I really scared them, because they both went running for my room. I felt bad for scaring them, so I rolled around on the floor wrestling with them when I noticed that they both had stolen some Halloween candy from the bag downstairs and figured that they were actually running to hide the candy from me. I don't like Milky Way bars anyway, so I didn't care that they had slobbered a few up. I think Mom gets candy to give out that we don't like so we won't eat it all before Halloween comes.

Frisky and Friskier looked so guilty that I left them in my room to enjoy their stolen loot. I forgot all about the fact that dogs aren't supposed to eat chocolate, but they were the small candy bars anyway.

The little kids in the neighborhood were going door to door before it was even dark. Their dads and moms were standing on the curb watching them go to the doors to trick-or-treat. Right before dark our doorbell rang. Mom said it was probably one of those early trick-or-treaters. She wasn't ready for them yet. She told me to stall them until she could empty the fun-sized candy bars into a big bowl.

I wondered why they called them 'fun size' when they were much smaller than the regular ones. Wouldn't 'fun size' be ten times the size of a regular candy bar?

I went to the door, but no one was there. Halloween pranksters were already out. I checked our two jack-o-lanterns to make sure no mean teenagers smashed them like they do every year. Nope, they were still sitting there glaring out. The one I carved was leering behind its evil glare and thousand tiny, sharp teeth, and Carl's was just smiling with the huge open gash that was supposed to be scary but got messed up when Kitty jumped up onto the table and bumped Carl's arm, so he ended up slicing too deep into the pumpkin. The knock also cut Carl's thumb, so blood poured all over the front of the pumpkin, which he thought was so cool and refused to wash off even though Mom told him to a thousand times.

I closed the door. "Just some teenagers playing ring and run," I shrugged.

"Oh, well." Mom sighed and went back to getting the house ready for a few of their friends who were coming over while she handed out candy.

Halloween was one of Mom's favorite holidays, and she was dressed up like some lady named Marilyn Monroe. Dad kept telling her she was the prettiest lady in the whole world, and that Marilyn Monroe would have been jealous of her. I liked it when Dad said that kind of stuff to Mom, because it always made her smile so big. Dad was dressed up like a nerd, or that's what he said anyway. As far as I could tell, he just put a big wad of white tape around the bridge of his glasses and pulled his pants higher so we both had high waters, only he meant to on account of that is what nerds do.

Mom's costume was much better than Dad's, really.

The doorbell rang again, and I was closest to the door. I ran to open it and no one was there, but I saw this tall guy sneaking to hide behind the bushes on the side of our house. I put my finger to my lips and motioned to Carl to follow me, and we tiptoed out

the back door. We crept in the darkening yard around the side and came up behind the crouching figure in the bushes. I would have been scared but I could hear the creature in the bushes chuckling and snorting, like he had just done the funniest thing in the world.

Carl motioned, to

me to follow him and then counted out, 'One... two... three' silently with his lips and fingers. At once we both sprang at the figure crouching low and tackled him.

He went facedown into the dirt and started sputtering, "Hey, you j-j-jerks, you m-messed up my costume!"

"ANDY!" both Carl and I said at the same time to the Frankenstein we had just tackled.

"Y-y-you knocked my b-b-bolts out, j-jerks!"

That was just a little of what we did. When he went facedown into the bushes and dirt, it smeared off half of his makeup. He actually looked scarier than a regular Frankenstein because it looked like his face was melting off.

"What are you trying to pull, dork?" Carl snarled at Andy.

"N-n-nothing, just having some f-f-fun." Andy seemed kind of scared of my brother.

"Well, don't do it again or I will knock you out."

But Carl didn't look too scary in the moonlight yet, because he wasn't wearing his werewolf stuff yet.

"Just relax, tough guy," I muttered under my breath.

"Oh yeah? What you going to do about it chicken-dracu-high-waters?" Carl snapped, popped me on the arm and started laughing in a ridiculous crazy man way.

I pulled on Andy's arm, ignoring my grumpy brother. "Come on Andy, my mom can fix your face."

"Nothing could fix that face, 'cept maybe a big bag over it!" Carl snarled and walked to the front yard.

Andy and I walked to the back and met Mom in the

kitchen. Mom turned and looked at Andy and screamed like she was really scared of him. Mom was pretty cool like that.

"Mrs. P-P-Peters, you look r-really pretty!" Andy mumbled. It was pretty obvious to everyone that my friend Andy had kind of a crush on my mom. His family wasn't so great, and my mom always made him feel like he was totally special to her.

"Thank you, Andy. You look very ghoulish tonight." Mom gushed.

"Yeah, my face was really c-c-ool before Carl and Gabe m-messed me up."

"Well, I can fix it up for you."

Andy beamed at mom's attention.

I felt sorry for him. It's kind of sad to watch a kid want a mom's attention so bad when you are used to just having it.

Mom fixed Andy's costume and makeup, and we were ready to head out for a night of fun and spooks. Carl was on the phone when we left, but it didn't sound like he was talking to one of his buddies. He was whispering and trying not to let us hear him. "I'll bet it's Denise," I told Andy.

"Yeah, l-l-let's l-listen on the upstairs phone..." Andy whispered a bit too loud.

"HANG ON!" Carl growled into the phone, cupping his hand around the receiver. He glared at us. "You guys touch that phone and I will give you both a major beating."

"Wow, G-Gabe, how do you l-l-live with him?" Andy whispered, this time quieter. "L-let's just g-g-go. He's no f-fun."

"BYE MOM! BYE DAD!" I yelled as Andy and I headed for the front door.

"Th-thank you Mrs. P-Peters."

Andy and I walked down the street, stopping at each house to trick-or-treat, and then decided to head up to the party they were having at the barn. We hardly know the Anderson people who own the farm, but the girl who is having the party goes to my brother's school, and from what people say has a raving crush on him. I don't understand why all of these girls are so interested in my brother all of a sudden. There were a bunch of older kids at the party, and we felt kind of awkward being there, so we decided to leave. As we were heading for the door I saw something that stopped me dead in my tracks. Carl and Denise were standing over by this big tank of water with a bunch of shiny red apples bobbing around.

Carl and Denise got their braces locked up while bobbing for apples. They were trying to work together to get the apple by pushing towards it and missing, and then their braces locked tight.

A bunch of people stood in a circle around them, some trying to help and some making loud catcalls about them K I S S I N G, chanting, "Carl and Denise, sitting in a tree, K I S S I N G... First comes...."

That's when Andy and I headed for the door. I didn't want Carl to even know I knew about this. It was just one of those things that would stay unspoken, until I needed to use it for blackmail.

"Let's just go trick-or-treat!" I yelled into the black night.

"Okay, sounds like a -p-plan! Hey, b-by the way, my d-dad's b-back."

"Annnndd...?"

"Well, h-he seems b-better. He's n-nicer anyway. Everyone was acting l-like he was a st-stranger until he told an old story h-he has t-t-told us a m-million times, which always cracks my b-big brothers up a l-l-lot more than me. After that it w-wasn't as t-t-tense."

"Is he going to be okay now?"

"M-Mom said she isn't holding her b-b-breath, but she's h-hopeful." I could see under the streetlight that Andy's eyes were full of tears, and he wiped his face with the back of his sleeve.

"Me too!" I patted Andy on the back and started running toward the streetlights where a hundred pounds of candy was waiting for us! We would go to Butch's house first, since his dad worked for a bubblegum company and they always gave away fistfuls.

CHAPTER SEVEN

Road Trip

Thanksgiving was only a week away. I could hardly stand the wait. Most people will say that Christmas is their favorite holiday, but Thanksgiving is my favorite. For one thing, Dad takes the days before Thanksgiving off to make the yearly trek to Kansas, so we can spend the night and wake up in my grandparent's farmhouse, which if you ask me, is the best place in the whole world to wake up.

As we got the last-minute things shoved into the trunk of mom's car, light snow began falling. Dad was singing, "It's beginning to look a lot like Christmas."

As I passed him, I thumped Dad on the arm, "Gosh Da-ad, it's not even Thanksgiving yet, don't rush it!"

"Doesn't everyone want Christmas to be every day?" Dad laughed.

"Not me. I want it to be Thanksgiving every day!"

"You would, you chicken-turkey-dork!" Carl shoved my shoulder as he passed me.

Dad and I both gave Carl a look, which said, that it makes no sense to combine two poultry to make an insult out of.

Mom locked the front door, slipped the key under the mat for Mrs. Morris, and we were on the road.

It isn't the turkey and stuffing and pie and all the other great junk we eat, it is that we go to my grandma and grandpa's farm in Kansas. It is the greatest place on earth. I love jumping out of the loft in the barn down into about twenty feet of hay, which Grandma stacks up special for us, even though she acts like it's no big thing. She is the kookiest lady you could ever meet! She always does stuff like that. She will go out of her way to make everything perfect or to do something really nice for someone, just because she knows they like it that way, and then she will totally slough it off, "Twern't nothin'. I would've had to of done it anyway; don't make a big thing of it."

Thing is, she did a lot of those kind of things that twern't nothin'. She tries to act really tough, but she is a big softy. But every year before we get there Dad has to remind us that, "Grandma is a bit crazy and who knows what she will have up her sleeve this year..." Then he and mom talk about how she isn't as crazy as Uncle Morris, and they compare how weird some of the aunts and uncles are.

Whenever we go to my grandparents' farm, we take Old Gold. That's what we all call Mom's car. It is an old Cadillac with wings on the back and it looks like the Batmobile if it were gold and fancy. We get to take all kinds of snacks, and Mrs. Morris feeds the animals while we're gone so I don't worry too much about them. Frisky and Friskier like Mrs. Morris, and Kitty and Flop kind of come and go as they please anyway, and half the time they are over in Mrs. Morris's backyard when we are home, so they don't really even notice we're gone. Mrs. Morris takes Squeaky and Squeakier over to her house to guinea-pig-sit, and I know they get taken care

of real good, because of the way she talks to them and pets them to make them squeal by scratching behind their ears.

The worst thing in the world, totally, is sitting next to my brother all the way through Colorado and Kansas! First of all, he always leans hard on me and puts his big stinky feet across my lap. No matter how many times I push them off, he just sticks them back on my lap and pushes down as hard as he can to keep them there and to show me who's boss. "Get your feet off me!" I would always say so everyone in the car could hear me, of course.

Under his breath Carl would growl, "What a chicken-tattle-tale! Mom-my, Dad-dy, I can't stand up for myself. I am a big chicken-baby!"

He would push the words into my ear so Mom and Dad couldn't hear him, and his nasty, hot breath would make me feel carsick, especially if he had just been eating some beef jerky or something. The absolute worst is when Mom makes boiled eggs for the road trip and Carl breathes his nasty egg breath on me. It smells like when Frisky has gas, and that is the worst!

This time, as we were rolling along past the three-millionth wheat field, Carl grabbed the Tiger Beat magazine out of my hand. "HEY LOOK, HERE'S THAT EDDIE WIMP THAT EVERYONE THINKS GABEY-BABY LOOKS LIKE!"

"GIVE IT BACK!" I screamed.

"MY LITTLE HOLLYWOOD CHICKEN-DORK BROTHER IS ON THE COVER! ISN'T THAT CUTE? HOW SWEET, GABY READS A GIRLIE MAGAZINE!" Carl taunted, pushing his elbows into my side.

"Carl, give Gabe back his magazine, and just leave him alone! It's not a girl's magazine!" Mom glared at him.

"Yeah, right!" Carl rolled his eyes.

"Keep your hands to yourself! Can you do that for one minute?"

Mom turned all the way around to show him she meant business.

I held the magazine up in victory for having gotten Carl in trouble. Mom looked at it and said, "Wow, honey, you do look like this kid."

"Yeah, honey, you do, you big chicken-wuss," Carl mocked in a low voice he thought only I could hear, but Mom gave him one of those looks that kills.

One of Carl's specialties was to lean into my space and burp* as loud as he could. He always somehow convinced Mom and Dad to let him drink pop, which was like setting a burp bomb off in the backseat of the car. He thinks he is so funny trying to say the alphabet in burp language and blowing his hot breath on me, pushing the burp into my nose between every letter, "ABURP - blow, BBURP - blow, CBURP - blow, DBURP - blow...."

By about H, I think I was going to hurl as his carbonated

*Burp - everyone knows what a burp is, but I thought it was funny that it was in the dictionary. It's a verb that means to noisily release air from the stomach through the mouth; belch. BUT, did you know there was a thing called a 'burp gun?' It is a noun for a lightweight submachine gun. BUT, there may be a burp gun, but there is no such thing as a belch gun.

jerky breath covered the whole inside of the car like a big, brown cloud.

"Carl, stop it right now..." said my defender.

Mom tried to say it all serious, but you can tell she is laughing, which just encourages him to keep going. Carl doesn't take her too seriously, because she always thinks it is funny, but then again, it isn't her face he is breathing into.

"Da-ad, he's doing it again!" I will say for the hundredth time in an hour, and Dad will say goofy stuff like, "DO YOU BOYS WANT ME TO STOP THIS CAR? OH NO, I DON'T THINK YOU DOOOOO!" and then he'd growl like he is really steamed at us. It takes a lot to get Dad really mad. I have only seen it a couple times, and I will tell you, I don't want to see it again.

Carl usually says something smart like, "Oh, yeah, Dad, then what. You are going to give me a spanking?" he will say it in a sweet voice like he is kidding, but I can tell he is really trying to see how Dad will react since no one has really spanked him in a lot of years. Just once I wish Dad would do just that - stop the car, pull Carl out of the backseat, and for the whole world to see, give him a spanking that would keep him from sitting down - which is impossible anyways because he can't stand in the car all the way to Kansas.

But like usual, Dad just glared in the rearview mirror, trying to put on a real mean face, which never really seems mean at all. "CARL, IF I HAVE TO TELL YOU AGAIN TO LEAVE GABE ALONE, I'M GOING TO DUMP YOU ON THE SIDE OF THE HIGHWAY AND LEAVE YOU THERE!"

"UH HUH... COME ON DAD, DO IT! ANYTHING'S BETTER THAN RIDING BACK HERE WITH CHICKEN-GUT-LESS!"

"Carl, be nice!" Mom tried again.

Carl moaned, "Man, living with this little chicken-twit is pure torture. Can't we just leave him off at the next truck stop...?"

Carl went back to his burp and blow.

You see, the thing is, even though sometimes it seems like Dad is actually annoyed, he would never do any of the stuff he says he would, so Carl never really listens to him, and just goes back to annoying me - "HBURP - blow, IBURP - blow...

Mom rolled her eyes and turned up the radio, which is just a bunch of static with voices fading in and out as we pass through little towns. Why do people want to hear all that stuff about wheat and bugs and stuff you can spray on your pets if they have ticks or fleas or chiggers?

"Mom, what's a chigger?" I said, leaning as far away from Carl as I could.

"It's a nasty little bug that goes under your skin and makes you itch like the devil."

I thought about making a comment about how that sounded a lot like Carl, but I didn't need one more of his punches on the bicep, which of course most of the time leaves a frog bubble.

"The devil itches?" I teased Mom.

"Okay smarty, why did you ask about chiggers?" Mom looked at me in the rear view mirror.

"Dunno. Just something I heard on the radio."

Just about the time I was getting ready to figure out some way to open Carl's car door and launch him out, we stopped at this truck stop to get gas and to go to the bathroom. And there something really funny happened to him.

Dad always taught us to open the bathroom door with our foot, to flush with our foot, and to turn the water on and off in the sink with our foot. It's really kind of funny to hop around on one foot in the bathroom, trying to use our feet like hands but Dad says there are a billion germs on all of the surfaces in there that could make us really sick, so we don't touch anything. First you use the bottom of your shirt to open the door, so you don't have to touch the handle, and then once you are inside your feet work like hands.

In the bathroom there were three stand-up toilets, two tall ones for men and the other one short for little kids. Carl shoved me towards the mini one so he could use the "big boy's": "You haven't earned the right to use the MEN'S yet, chicken-squeak."

"Whatever..." I muttered under my breath.

Well, when Carl went to flush the handle with his foot, I guess his pants were too tight, because he couldn't quite get his leg high enough. Right when this big cowboy trucker guy came in, Carl gave it another big kick to try to flush the handle, and when he did his other foot gave way on account of the floor was all wet. Carl started to fall back and his leg got caught in the toilet and he was just hanging there with his foot lodged in the toilet and his head and shoulder on the ground.

The big cowboy guy jumped over there and tried to help him get his foot unstuck, but somehow dork-head's tennis shoe had lodged into the corner of the urinal, and Carl started screaming at the top of his lungs, "DON'T PULL! DON'T TWIST! OUCH!" He was screaming so loud that Dad came rushing in to the bathroom. That must have been a funny sight for Dad, my brother stuck in a toilet and a big old cowboy dude trying to yank him out.

I was doubled over laughing hard when Mom came in too. There wasn't enough room in the bathroom for three people, let alone five, and now the manager of the gas station was coming in, and several other people who had been waiting to use the bathroom were looking in to see what all the commotion was about. Carl's face was beet red, and once Dad and the cowboy unhooked him, he skulked out like a beaten dog.

The funniest part was when Mom insisted Carl change his clothes: "Who knows what on heaven's earth was on that bathroom floor. Look at you, you are all wet!"

Today in a truck stop bathroom
In the toilet Carl stuck his shoe.
When in walked a HUGE cowboy.
He laughed so hard his face was blue!

So Carl had to get clothes out of his suitcase, and Dad helped him take a paper towel bath in the men's room, and then change his clothes, all while it was like zero degrees out.

For the next twenty miles in the car, Carl didn't move a muscle and I didn't dare say a word, but every so often, I just couldn't help it: a laugh would explode right out of my nostrils. Carl just kicked me or leaned on me with his stupid sharp elbows when that happened, but the scene in my head of Carl standing in the bathroom in his underwear shivering while Dad washed him down with paper towels just cracked me up so much.

We were getting close to my grandparent's farm and I was ready to be anywhere but in the car. I whispered in the meanest voice I could make, "Someday, I am going to be big and I am going to make you eat that elbow!" I said as Carl pressed his elbow into my ribcage again.

"Oh, I am so scared... Check this out!" He held his hand up straight parallel with the floor. "You know what this is?"

I mouthed the word along with him, "Controlled fear, that's what." "Hmmm, haven't heard that stupid joke a thousand times before," I sneered. That's when Carl pushed his whole body on top of mine and did the most disgusting thing ever, right on me.

"MOMMMMMMMMM!"

"Would you two please stop it!" she exclaimed.

"Us two? Did you see what he did?" I complained.

Dad growled, "Well, I sure smell what he did!" And with that, Dad hit the electric windows, and the entire car flooded with icy cold air.

If you think I got cold, Carl was still damp from his bathroom accident.

CHAPTER EIGHT

My Crazy Grandma

As we got closer to the farmhouse, Dad started to talk about how crazy Grandma was, and that we should be ready for anything. It's funny Mom felt like she had to defend her. Carl made some comment about what a loony-tune Gran was, but that is what made me like her more than just about anyone else I knew.

When we pulled up the long gravel road to Grandma's farm, I held my binoculars up to see if Gran was waiting on the porch like she did every time we came to see her. Yup, I could see her up there on the front porch, her long crazy hair blowing around her head all wild, and her overalls loose and bunchy. No matter how many times she pushed her glasses up her nose, they were always hanging on the tip. She was holding two large objects -which seemed to have lives of their own - straight up parallel with the ground.

Carl snarled, "What's Grandma doing now?"

I didn't like his tone. He and Gran didn't get along like she and I did. As far as I was concerned, the world could use a whole bunch more people like Gran.

"Shut up Grumpio-Carlio," I yelled, then opened the car door and jumped out and started running up the road to meet her.

As I got closer I saw what she was holding. Clutched in each hand were two chickens. She began to spin her arms around in big, arcing, pinwheel motions. The chickens were squawking and flapping their wings wildly, and then after about five turns they were silent.

"Supper!" Gran yelled, looking at the chickens and then at my horrified face. "GRAN!" I choked out.

"Well, young man, where do you think your favorite fried chicken comes from for your chicken-fried mashed potatoes, chicken gravy and chicken-speckled dumplings? Now get over here and give me a hug, youngen! My oh my, look at you. You are a foot taller and a yard more handsome than the last time I saw you!" When Gran hugged me, I could feel her bony hands pressing against my back as well as the two dead chickens.

I still felt kind of shocked at what I had just seen. "Gran, how can you...?"

"They aren't pets, Gabriel, they're food. I'm sorry if that upset you, but it is a fact of farm life."

"I know... but isn't there some way?"

"Hmmm, well, let's see... NOPE!" Gran started laughing into the wind.

I scrunched up my eyebrows and stared at the chickens that were now just hanging there like stuffed animals.

The car pulled up the icy gravel drive, and then Mom, Dad and Carl got out. Carl walked up to Gran and hugged her. "Hey!"

"Hey, yourself! That's just something the horses eat, not a way to greet one's favorite grandma!" She rubbed Carl's head hard and tried to give him a hug.

He pulled away and stared at her like she was from a different planet. Before she could notice, Mom was hugging on her.

"Jerk! Why can't you just be nice?" I sneered at Carl under my breath.

"Shut up and mind your own beeswax*, chicken-butt!"

"Carl! Gabe! Start plucking!" Gran said, throwing the limp chickens at our feet. Their blank red eyes just stared at me. With that, she and my parents disappeared into the house with the suitcases.

Now, most grandmas just meet their grandsons with a hug or a kiss. Mine met me with dead meat.

Anyone who doesn't know my grandma would probably

*beeswax (noun), 1. wax secreted by bees to make honeycombs. 2. informal, a person's concern or business: that's none of your beeswax.

think she is a "crazy old coot," like my dad sometimes says, but he is just kidding around. She isn't like anyone else's grandma I know.

Whenever I tell the guys about her they say they think she sounds cool, and they all wish they had a grandma like her. I can't wait until next summer, because my grandma is coming to stay with us for a long time. She is the kind of grandma who will climb up into the tree house with us and go fishing and hunting, too.

You know how some grandparents tell you stories about when they were young and they always have a lesson to go with it? My grandma tells lots of stories, but never really to teach anything, just to share her history. No one could tell a "yarn" like my Gran. She tells me that I had her gift for storytellin'. I hope she's right.

I was standing in the kitchen watching Gran pulling the feathers off the chickens that we had missed when she nodded her head and told me to come up right close to her. I grabbed a chair and stood on it next to the sink where she was standing.

"Gabe, your dad said I might have upset you twirling those chickens that way."

"Nah, it wasn't a big d...."

"Young man, let me finish."

Gran looked at me and she seemed more gentle than I had ever seen her. "I would never do anything to scare you or put you off. You are one of my favorite people in the whole world! I was trying to be funny, and maybe it wasn't the right time or place." Grandma wiped her hand on her apron and lifted my chin so I was looking right in her eyes. "I know how much you love animals, and I do too! I treat these chickens and all of my animals better than most and they have a good life, but they are for food, and that some-times is a hard thing for city slickers to understand."

"I ain't no city slicker." I muttered.

"Now why you talking like that, boy? You have the best sense of grammar of anyone I know, and I should know, since I'm your grammer... Get it? Your grammer?"

"Ha ha. Not funny, Gran."

"Well, kind of funny. But I mean it. If that bothered you, you need to tell me."

"No, Gran, it's really okay. I mean, I feel bad for the chicken and all, but I do like your chicken and dumplings. I mean, I'm not a veterinarian or anything like that."

Gran looked at me real curious-like, like she wasn't sure if I knew the difference between the word 'veterinarian' or 'vegetarian.' I didn't let on either way.

She showed me how to make dumplings, and we talked and laughed for a long time.

My grandma often just sits on her front porch with a loaded shotgun waiting to pick off the 'dad-gum-varmints' that hunker down in her garden patch and do away with all of her prized vegetables. Her main targets are the bunny rabbits and the squirrels that steal away her favorite vegetables and her peaches and apples. Those varmints* are lucky to make it to another summer or autumn if they are anywhere near Grandma's shotgun's sites.

The first time I ever knew about her shotgun and her hunting ways was several years ago, when we went to the farm for Thanksgiving.

We had been there a few hours when she told me she wanted me to meet her out on the porch, so I could tell her all the things that were going on in my life.

*varmint (noun), 1. a troublesome wild animal, esp. a fox. 2. a troublesome and mischievous person, esp. a child. ORIGIN mid 16th cent.: alteration of vermin.

The wind was blowing and it was freezing cold out there, but Grandma was rocking in her chair with a blanket wrapped around her shoulders. As I walked out there, she motioned for the other chair.

"Grandma, it's freezing out here!"

"You need to toughen up, city-slicker!" She fake-growled and pushed her glasses up her nose.

That was kind of funny, since we lived out in the country too, but not nearly as country as Grandma's farm I guess. "B-But..."

Grandma interrupted, "Everyone's got a butt and they're good for one thing... sittin' on. Now sit down on yours, and tell me what has been going on with you."

I started to tell her about school and other stuff. "Well, my friend Andy and I have this..."

Grandma seemed to be talking to herself as I was talking, "Dad-gummit, that doggone thing is gonna...

"Grandma...?"

"Go on now, tell me what you and Andy were doing...." But she wasn't even looking at me when she talked to me. She was scrunching her face up real tight, like she had just bitten down on something really sour.

I started again, "Well, we have this tree house where our club meets, and we wanted to spend some of our allowances on some carpet..."

"You are gonna die, you little son of a gun..." Grandma started smacking her lips together all crazy-like.

"Grandma? Who're you talking to?" It was shocking hearing my grandma say the same kind of stuff Carl said to me.

Grandma had a far-off look on her face, because she was looking out into her front yard. I looked to where she was staring, but didn't see anything. All of a sudden she whipped around behind her rocking chair and pulled out this long, double-barreled, shotgun and raised it up to her shoulder. She was crouching in front of her chair now.

"Grandma, what are you..."

BOOM! BOOM! Two deafening shots echoed across the yard, and in the snow dusting the yard from the blowing wind was a red blotch where just seconds before a furry little rabbit had been.

"Grandma? Wh-what, why..."

Carl came running from the barn where he was helping my dad and grandpa with something. "Cool, can I shoot it? Can I?" Grandma nodded at Carl.

Then Mom came out, "What in heaven's name was that noise?"

Dad and Grandpa were standing in the door of the barn watching the commotion.

Grandma ignored Mom's question. "Well, finally, Mr. Carrot Snatcher. I guess your gardening days are done!"

She smacked her lips, patted her shotgun like you'd pat a dog, and set it back behind her chair, like it was something that happened in every porch conversation.

Mr. McGregor flashed through my mind, and I wondered if the rabbit Grandma had just blown to bits was like Peter Rabbit.

Gran looked at me over her glasses. "Gabriel, I spent all last summer chasing those doggone rabbits off of my lettuce and spinach and then the varmints started digging down and eaten the tops of my carrots, which let in the worm rot... I think that is finally the last of 'em. Now I gotta make sure the squirrels get it too, or I won't see any peaches come summer. You do like my peach preserves, now don't cha?"

"Yuh..." My mind was reeling. Did my grandma actually just blow two big shotgun holes into a tiny little bunny rabbit? Then I thought about how cool it would be to shoot her double barrel shotgun. Like usual, I was too young though, and it just ate me up to watch Grandma out there later showing Carl how to hold it so it didn't knock his shoulder off when it kicked back.

Carl held it up and aimed it at the scarecrow Gran had set back up in her vegetable garden. When Carl pulled the trigger he flew back onto his butt, the gun firing off into nowhere. The scarecrow was safe when it came to Carl, but if I got a chance WATCH OUT!

Dad and Grandpa were watching, too. Dad said, "Do you think we should go help?"

"Would you dare?" Grandpa started laughing, and motioned for my dad to follow him into the barn.

So, this year was my year to shoot the shotgun. Since that day on the porch a couple years ago, I myself had shot and skinned over ten rabbits with a twenty-two rifle and a high-powered pellet gun and was secretly making a coat for my mom, but the more I thought about it, the more I thought my grandma would like it even better. Maybe I could get it all finished by next summer and give it to her when she stayed with us.

CHAPTER NINE

The Hayloft Incident

One of my favorite things to do on the farm is to jump out of the hayloft. Grandma piles the hay up so deep below the loft that you can dive right off and never get hurt. The problem is, like usual, Carl thinks it is the funniest thing to torment me. He chases me up the ladder and tries to throw me off.

When I was little he always hurled me off before I could throw myself off. But now my leg is much better, and I think I can outrun him.

I was climbing into the loft when Carl came rushing into the barn.

"I'm going to pitch you off!" he yelled.

"No you aren't!" I got to the top, and started wiggling my hips and taunting him, "You can't get me! You can't get me! CARLIO THE KING OF FARTHEAD'S A BIG LOSER!"

I noticed my breath coming out because of the cold, but I didn't feel the cold from moving around so much.

"You are so dead you chicken-turd!"

Carl was breathing really hard, and the white breath coming out of his mouth looked like a vicious dragon's breath. When I saw his big, ugly face at the top of the steps, I threw my body off into the hay in a sort of sideways flip.

I screamed, "COWABUNGA, SLOWPOKE!" and went sailing through the air like an eagle. As soon as I hit the hay, I started swimming in it as fast as I could to the ladder, because Carl would surely jump right on top of me and then do something stupid like the spit yoyo*, the worst kind of torture! I wasn't going to let him try it on me again, not if I could help it.

I got to the bottom of the ladder right as he landed about five feet away from me.

"I'm gonna kill you, Gabey-baby!" He always got so frustrated when I outsmarted him or foiled his plan to pulverize me.

"Not if you can't catch me!"

I repeated the same routine, waiting just long enough for him to see me swan-dive off gracefully into the hay, directing my body closer to the ladder this time.

Carl got into position quickly and this time tried to land right on top of me. I got the jump on him again, and swam right to the ladder and climbed it as fast as I could.

"YOU CAN'T CATCH ME! YOU CAN'T CATCH ME!" I chanted as I dove again into the hay and then rolled, flipped my body out of the hay.

"LOSER!" I screamed and ran out the front barn door and disappeared down near the pond as fast as I could. I was lying

*The spit yoyo: What he would do is catch me and hold me down on my back and then work up a gob of spit in his mouth. Then with my arms pinned up by my shoulders and held down by his knees, he would let the string of spit out of his mouth for a couple inches, suck it back, drop it down a little closer, suck it back, closer, and suck it back. Sometimes he didn't suck it back in time, and a nasty glob of spit would land in my eye or on my cheek. Like I said, the worst torture known to little brothers anywhere!

beneath a broken stump, breathing into my sweater so my breath wouldn't be seen, and watching Carl as he ran along the little path that the stream followed to the pond.

He stopped about three feet from me, but thankfully didn't see me. The breath was steaming out of his mouth as he yelled, "YOU CHICKEN-IDIOT, WHEN I CATCH YOU, YOU'LL BE SORRY! I'M GONNA CREAM YOU!"

His voice echoed off the barn, across the water and probably into the next town over. I shuddered at the thought of what Carl would do to me if he caught me. He was really angry.

It was then I noticed that I had left tracks all the way to the stump that Carl somehow missed. I was lucky he wasn't too smart.

When I was pretty sure Carl had found something else to do or someone else to torment, I climbed out from the hollow in the big stump and skittered toward the house, staying low. I followed Grandpa around, staying close by while we did some chores, knowing my brother would never bother me with Grandpa around. Then he went in to "catch the news."

It was getting kind of dark, and it was cold. I bustled into the kitchen where Gran and my mom were working on dinner. "Anyone seen Carl?"

"No hon, he said he was going to go up to Roger's." Mom murmured, paying more attention to what Gran was doing than me.

Roger lived on the next farm up the gravel road. He and Carl had become friends last year, when they found they both had a fondness for stupid wrestling. Roger's dad had once been a professional wrestler before he was a farmer, and told them all kinds of stories.

"Good!" I exclaimed with relief.

They both looked at me curiously, but ignored my comment.

"WOMAN, get me some more tea!" my grandpa barked from the parlor.

"Get off your duff and get it yourself, OLD MAN!" Gran growled.

Mom looked at me and rolled her eyes.

"I'll get it for you, Daddy!"

"Don't you dare!" Gran growled at my mom. "He can move his tired, old bones, and get his own tea."

"Look at how lovely the sunset is, Mom?" my mom said to Gran, obviously trying to change the subject.

Grandpa puttered into the kitchen and gave Gran a peck on the cheek, and then pulled open the fridge door, poured himself a glass of iced tea and puttered back into the parlor. "You don't know how to sweeten it right anyway, old woman!" Grandpa said, chuckling to himself.

Gran rolled her eyes and snapped a towel at Grandpa, barely missing him.

"Why does Grandpa drink iced tea all the time, even in the winter?" I wondered aloud.

"Hmmmm..." Gran seemed lost in thought somewhere. "Cuz he's an old coot, that's why!"

"Gran, why don't you like Grandpa?" I squeaked.

"WHAT? What kind of a thing is that to say?"

"Well, you talk kind of mean to him."

"Sonny boy, when you have been married as long as I have, we'll have us a talk. Until then, just button yer little lip." She rubbed my head to show me she was just kidding me. "I love that old man more'n just bout anything I've ever loved. But, you gotta learn how to keep 'em in line, now don't you?"

I just shrugged. I had no idea what she was talking about, and I was sorry I brought it up right then.

Mom just smiled at me and winked.

CHAPTER TEN

Cats, Rats and Bats

The sky in Kansas looked really different than it did at home because it was so flat. Everything turned a dark red when the sun was setting. I was used to seeing the sunset up by the mountains, but the mountains were nowhere to be seen on the long, rolling prairie land.

"Gran, may I go back to the barn for some more jumpin'?"

"Supper's in fifteen minutes, so you can get in some jumpin', but you need to get back here in time to warsh up for supper. YOU KNOW HOW THE OLD COOT DOESN'T LIKE TO BE KEPT WAITING!" she said loud enough for Grandpa to hear.

Grandpa chuckled. "Pipe down, old woman! I can't hear the man on the television over your loud bellowing!" he answered from the parlor where he and Dad were still watching some boring old news show.

"YOU BE CAREFUL OUT THERE!" Gran yelled.

"I will!" I pulled a scarf around my neck, and put my winter coat and some mittens on.

"Careful for that mean old barn monster!" was the last thing I heard Gran say as I closed the front door.

A shiver ran up my spine. Then I ran through the darkening farmyard as fast as I could, watching over my shoulder for my big brother. When I entered the barn I shivered, part from the cold and part because it was getting pretty dark in here. Orangeish-red light streamed in through the cracks between the boards, and left long bars of dusty light across the hay. It felt a lot spookier in there when it was dark and when I was alone.

I pushed the big, creaky barn doors shut so Carl wouldn't know I was here, and left the light off just in case, even though I would be a lot more comfortable with a bright, glaring light burning. The smell of hay and some kind of musky scent wafted through the still air. Suddenly the silence seemed louder than anything. I started to climb the ladder to the loft when I heard a skittering noise across wood - overhead, I thought, but I couldn't really tell where it had come from.

"Probably just a barn cat," I said out loud, trying to convince myself. Then I heard more sounds, more human or monster I thought. They sounded like muffled, evil laughter. But I thought of the times Gran had said, "Barns are full of 'cats, rats and bats,' and shrugged the noises off as one of those. None of those animals seemed scary to me.

As I neared the top of the ladder though, I heard a low, deep growling sound. I couldn't tell if it were below, above me or next to me. The sun had gone down, and the streams of dusty light were fading fast, making it quickly dark in there. I wondered if this had been such a good idea, and longed for the warm kitchen that smelled of Gran's great cooking.

The growling began to get louder.

"Who's there?" More growling, and an evil cackling laughter ricocheted off the walls. I could tell there were two of whatever it was in the barn with me because four eyes were staring at me.

Whatever they were, they were way too close for comfort, and I was terrified.

"GRRRRRRRRRR."

The growl echoed off the walls inside the barn and, I still couldn't tell where it was coming from.

"Hello?" I was frozen in place. Was the growling below me? If so, I didn't want to jump into it. Was the growling up there in the loft with me? If so, I needed to get out of there.

"GRRRR, RRRRRRR, MMMMMMM." It got louder and scarier. Were they Zombies? Aliens? Barn beings? Giant rats or the Barn Monster?

My chin was quivering, and a shiver, both cold and hot at the same time, moved up my back. I didn't know what to do. I couldn't tell where the sounds were coming from.

I crept to the edge of the loft, squinting hard, trying to see whatwas in the growing darkness and fully expecting to see evil green or red

I was so scared I simply couldn't move.

"GRRRRRRRRRRRRRRRR, BOO-HA-HA..." The growling and laughter was getting louder and definitely sounded closer.

"HELP!" the word weakly spilled out my mouth before I could stuff it back down. I wasn't really even calling for anyone, but suddenly I realized I had just indicated exactly where I was in the dark for the monster in the barn to attack.

My mind was racing. If I jumped as hard as I could, I would still be a long way from the barn door, but maybe I could make a run for it before the barn monster got me. Then, added to the growl was the sound of something moving right behind me, a scratching sound on the loft wood. And now it seemed to be coming toward me for sure.

I got ready to leap. I had turned to try to see behind me in the now almost-black barn. A huge chill swept up my back, and I realized I was wet with sweat from shivering out of fear.

"GRRRRR! ARGHHHHHHH!" Suddenly a large body flew out of the hay behind me, side-tackling me and throwing me out of control.

My body went spinning off the edge at a sideways angle. "AHHH!"

Right before my head collided with something really hard I heard Carl laughing from above.

"I told you I was going to get you, chicken-creep! You should be careful who you go around calling a loser!"

My head had hit the edge of the ladder and knocked me to the ground hard. I just lay there in the soft hay with a throbbing headache, but very relieved to realize the monster in the dark was just my big brother. "UHHHHHNNNN."

Carl kept laughing, "I am going to dive right on top of you and pulverize you, you chicken-little-weirdo.

Carl flew out of the loft and landed right next to me and then started to pull up on my underwear, "ATOMIC WEDGIE* FOR THE CHICKEN-LOSER!" he screamed.

I heard someone else up in the loft laughing hard and saying, "GRRRRRRRRRRR. THAT WAS PRICELESS!"

Then Carl's breath was going right up my nostril as he bore his elbow hard into my back.

Before I could figure out who was up in the loft, the barn doors burst open and a huge beam of light flooded in on us. I could see the outline of grandma against the now almost completely faded sunset. Gran must have heard all of my screaming from the house when she went out on the porch to call us in for dinner.

What she saw was Carl on top of me pushing me down into the hay and pulling my underwear up almost around my ears.

She screamed, "GET OFF'A HIM RIGHT NOW, YA BULLY!" Grandma could move fast when she wanted to. Carl sprung up off of me. The look on his face in the beam of light was that of pure terror, and then he was falling out of the hay pile, rolling down into the dirt at Gran's feet.

*Atomic wedgie (noun), an uncomfortable tightening of the underpants between the buttocks, typically produced when someone pulls the underpants up from the back as a practical joke. The use of the word 'atomic' with 'wedgie' makes it just that much bigger!

"We were just playin', Grandma. R-right, Gabe?"

I rolled away from Carl's iron grip and found my footing on the barn's dirt floor.

I whispered, "You are a dead man!"

"Twasn't what it sounded like to me!" Gran snarled.

"It's a game we play called chicken, where I..." Carl attempted to make her less mad.

"Don't you lie to me, young man!" Gran growled.

"BUT..."

"DON'T YOU 'BUT' ME! TURN AROUND, YOUNG MAN!"

"WHAT? WHY" I, UH..." Before Carl knew what was happening, Gran had pulled him to his feet, turned him around and was lifting her hand up high to paddle him.

HA HA
In the barn I got a
wedgie
Carl pulled my undies to
my ear!
But Gran gave him a
whooping
He won't be sitting that
much is clear!

MY UNDER WEAR

Carl hadn't had a spanking in a long time, and now my grandma, who was probably half a foot shorter than him, was giving him what-for!

As I pulled my own underwear, from my atomic wedgie* out of my crack, I started running for the house, but as I did I saw Roger throwing himself out of the window of the loft down onto the bales of hay that were outside leaning up on the barn for the cattle and then skittering into the darkness before my grandma could get a hold of him, too.

Later Carl sat sulking at the table for dinner, totally silent. No one asked what had happened, and as much as I wanted to tell them, I didn't dare. Not yet, anyway.

CHAPTER ELEVEN

Not Miss Sally!

The day before Thanksgiving Gran walked me out to the chicken coop. The chickens were running around free in a space that was fenced off for them.

There were some really colorful chickens with black and white feathers and bright red eyes. They were my favorites. They would sometime scratch in the dirt and then start jumping at each other.

Anyway, Gran took me out there and gave me a bucket of grain to throw for the chickens.

As I was feeding them, Gran cracked the ice off of the water trough and then suddenly barked, "GABEY, PICK ONE!" (It was a bit windy, so we had to yell to be heard.)

I thought about the two chickens she had twirled into oblivion* when we first showed up, and a shiver ran up my spine. "WHY?" I wished she didn't call me that anymore.

"PICK ONE!"

"GRAN, WHAT'RE YOU UP TO?"

*oblivion (noun), obscurity, limbo, anonymity, nonexistence, nothingness.

"IF YOU DON'T PICK ONE SOON, I WILL PICK ONE, AND YOU DON'T WANT ME TO PICK ONE OF YOUR FAVORITES, DO YOU? HOW 'BOUT MISS SALLY THERE?"

All of a sudden I knew what this was about. "NO GRAND-MA! NOT MISS SALLY!"

Miss Sally had last year been a chick that I helped. Grandma had threatened to get rid of her because she was a sickly runt. I told her I wanted to keep her, and named her after a nice lady who used to baby-sit me at the time. Miss Sally had a funny heart-shape on her back that had grown with her, so she was easy to tell apart.

Gran smiled slyly. We both knew she would never hurt Miss Sally. She had become more of a pet, which was totally against "Farm Rules," as Gran called them.

"Okay then, city slicker, pick another. PICK TWO!"

Overhead a murder of crows** flew squawking loudly, and then landed in the cornfield next to the barn, making a huge noise as they pecked around on the ground for some of the cornstalks poking through the snow from what was left from the harvest months ago. "Where's my shotgun when I need it?" Gran muttered to herself.

I half-heartedly picked out two plump chickens that usually stayed over by the shed and didn't seem to have much personality - unlike like Miss Sally, who would greet me when I went out there by running around in circles and pecking at the dirt right next to my feet. When I talked to her, she seemed to be listening, but she just nodded her head up and down. Sometimes it's nice to talk to someone or something that seems to agree with everything you say.

Grandma ran up to one of them and suddenly grabbed it

** *murder of crows* - *A flock of crows is actually called a murder of crows.*

by the neck, then she grabbed the other one in her other hand. She held them both up shoulder-high and started to twirl them - not exactly twirl them around, but twirl their necks around. Then they started flying around in an arc.

"GRANDMA!"

"What?"

"How can you do that?"

"Do what?"

"GRANDMA, YOU JUST...."

We stepped into the chicken coop, away from the wind.

"We've talked about this. You liked my special chicken-and-dumplin's with 'tatoes and brown gravy last night, didn't you?"

"Yes," I squeaked.

"Wait'll you get a load of my chicken enchilada pie t'night!"

"But, Gran, why do you have to strangle them like that?"

"It's the merciful way, Gabe. They don't even know what hit 'em."

Gran then squeezed the head of one of the chickens with her thumb and forefinger, and with the other hand pulled hard, removing its head from its body. She then dropped the body. It ran around weakly, blood spurting out in an arc, and then it just moved around like it was chicken-dancing.

"That's why they say, 'runnin around like a chicken with its head cut off!'" Gran laughed deep in her throat.

I blinked hard, not believing what I had just seen again.

She did the same with the other chicken, and the two of

them collided in the small pen and fell over, but kicked up in the air, like they were still alive.

Gran grabbed up one of the chickens again, and tossed one of the heads into the chicken pen. All of a sudden, all of the chickens pounced and were fighting over the head.

"THEY'RE CANNIBALS, GRAN!"

"They're so stupid, they'll eat just bout anything," Gran muttered.

I was still reeling at the way Gran had just pulled the chicken's head off.

"Grandma, that seems so cruel."

She just nodded. "Well, city slicker, it's actually fast, they don't feel a thing. When did you get so sensitive? And where else do you think those chickens in my yummy cooking came from?"

"Safeway?"

"Boy, you need to come live here on the farm one of these summers and get a reality check on things. Your momma is raisin' you up to be a softy."

That hurt my feelings.

Gran peered at me through her glasses, which had slipped

so far to the end of her nose that they were almost in her mouth. My grandma was a "tough old bird," as Grandpa would say, but when she needed to be nice, she could. I guess she realized she had hurt my feelings because she dropped the other chicken and then wrapped her arms around me and squeezed me tight.

"I'm sorry, Gabey, I was just kiddin' you. Not about coming to live here, I would love that, but about being a softy. You are a tough kid!"

She kissed the top of my head and kept squeezing me tight. Then as quickly as she hugged me, she let me go.

"Okay now, pluck those chickens so we can make us some good gizzard soup." She laughed and walked back up the small path to the house, leaving me alone with two dead chickens and no idea really how to pluck them right, since I slipped into the house the night before and left Carl to pluck them by himself.

"And don't call me 'Gabey,' either," I said to nobody but the chickens. "Hey guys, my brother always calls me chicken, too. He thinks it's a big insult, but I don't care."

Of course the two dead chickens had very little to say about the subject.

I noticed one of the chicken's heads lying there on the top of one of the chicken pens. I wrapped some straw around it and stuffed into my back pocket. You never know when it might come in handy up in the attic when I tell Carl a scary story about a ghost chicken.

After I had tried to pull a feather out of one of them for about thirty seconds with no luck, I remembered that these chickens weren't going to be feeling anything, and then I started yanking the feathers out and throwing them around. It looked like it was snowing inside the chicken coop.

Two chickens were watching me with blank stares. I wondered if they were mad at me for what I was doing. I got the very last feather off the second chicken, and somehow knew it was going to make Gran proud of me.

I ran, twirling the chickens by their feet, as I headed up the path. The last of the blood made a droplet trail behind me.

Carl was going the other way down the path. "What are you doing, chicken-boy?"

I held the chickens up in Carl's face and began to run again toward the house. "I'M GOING TO SHOW GRAN THE BALD CHICKENS! DON'T GO NEAR THE CHICKEN YARD, EVERYTHING DOWN THERE HAS GONE BALD! GRAMPS SAID THERE'S SOMETHING IN THE WATER!"

I would have paid a million dollars to have a picture of the face my brother was making, because all of a sudden my brother fidgeted with his hair all of the time. I think it has something to do with Denise, but he doesn't say much about that.

After one of the best Thanksgivings of my life, we were heading back home. Carl was leaning hard on me in the back seat, as usual.

I pushed on Carl's head hard. "Mom, what would you think of me going to live with Gran and Gramps for the summer?"

Mom and Dad looked at each other and smiled. "Well, I think when you are in middle school that might be a good idea, but I think it should wait until then, don't you?"

Carl said, "The sooner, the better, see you 'round, chicken-boy... I'll pack your bags when we get home!"

"Okay, SPANKY-BOY!"

We both knew what that meant.

"Or is it chicken-of-a-ghost-chicken-head?" That one cracked me up, since the chicken head had worked really well the other night in my story, when I talked about how it haunted farm-house attics and tossed the chicken head onto Carl's chest.

I haven't heard him scream like a girl for a long time.

CHAPTER TWELVE

Snow Days

When Dad called up the stairs for Carl and me to wake up and get moving, the scent of bacon coming from the kitchen smashed into my nose like a moving truck. My mouth began to water. There is nothing better than the smell of bacon frying in the morning, except for my dad's coffee smells really good, too, when it is percolating on the stove. But it doesn't taste like it smells; it just tastes like a big bowl of yuck. The bacon tastes just like it smells and is one of my favorite foods!

As I was changing out of my pajamas and pulling my pants on I started thinking about how the time between Thanksgiving and Christmas seems to take so long. You are just waiting for Christmas break and can hardly think of anything else, but school just drags on and on. The skies are all dark and cloudy and it is cold! cold! cold!

I like going down to the lake to skate and stuff like that, but it gets dark early and mom doesn't want us outside after dark when it is cold, so other than the weekends I don't get to see my buddies as much. I don't mind spending time in the house, and I like my bedroom and all, but sometimes I need something really exciting to happen.

So when I went down to the kitchen to get ready to go to school Dad was standing there at the stove frying eggs and bacon and making toast with a huge smile on his face. "Hello, Gabriel, would you like strawberry jam, or cinnamon sugar and butter, on your toast?"

"Hmmm... jam, please."

Dad was humming to the radio that sits in the windowsill where Flop likes to watch the world go by. Flop likes country music and sometimes meows to it. I often can hear Dad talking to Flop in the morning, and I like how much my dad likes my cat.

I crunched on a crispy piece of bacon, and both Frisky and Friskier sat right at my feet wagging their tails, hoping that I would share my bacon and eggs. I watched Dad dancing around while he was humming. He just cracks me up sometimes.

"What's up, Dad, you look too happy for a school day!"

"Oh come on, grumpy, school's not so bad, is it?" He nodded toward the newspaper that was sitting at his place at the breakfast table.

"Yeah, grumpy chicken-shorts!" Carl snarled sarcastically as he passed me on the way to the fridge and smacked the back of my head.

"Ow, Dad, Carl hit me!" I complained.

"Ow, Dad, Carl *hit* me!" Carl, mocked me.

"STOP COPYING ME!" I said purposely loud.

"Stop copying me!" Carl continued his mocking.

"Carl, keep your hands to yourself! Stop annoying your brother!"

Carl put on his most innocent look, "What? I didn't do...."

96

"Young man, I have eyes." Dad's tone changed to let Carl know he was serious.

Carl sulked. "Sorry," he muttered half-heartedly and ran his fingers through his hair for probably the hundredth time. He then looked at himself in the back of a spoon.

"Why don't you take a picture? It will last longer!" I whispered.

"Why don't you be a bigger wuss?" He whispered then he looked over to Dad, who was busy looking out the window and then punched me on the arm, raising a frog bubble.

"OW! DAD!"

I looked where Dad had nodded at the paper sitting at his place at the table. The headline on the front page of the newspaper should read; THREE DAYS OFF OF SCHOOL BECAUSE OF A HUGE BLIZZARD*! But what it said was, 'PREPARE FOR A GOOD OLD-FASHIONED BLIZZARD. BATTEN DOWN THE HATCHES!'

My dad's friend was the editor at the newspaper, and he was always writing goofy headlines, not the kind you see in real big town papers. That's why dad is in such a good mood, I thought to myself. No one likes a big storm as much as my dad!

Dad turned off the radio and flipped on the t.v. in the living room. The news people on t.v. started to talk about the blizzard coming in late this afternoon, and predicting that it wouldn't stop all the way through the weekend.

At school the blizzard was the topic of the day. The store across the street from school was jam-packed with cars and people

* blizzard (noun), a severe snowstorm with high winds and low visibility; snowstorm, whiteout, snow squall, snowfall; nor'easter, northeaster.

rushing in and then scurrying out with mounds of groceries in their carts, preparing for the GOOD OLD-FASHIONED BLIZZARD.

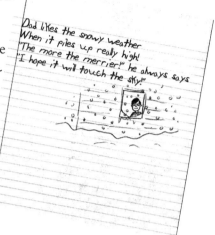

Dad likes the snowy weather
When it piles up really high!
"The more the merrier" he always says
"I hope it will touch the sky!"

On the way home, the lady that drives my carpool listened to the radio and kept telling us to look at the huge, gray clouds hovering over the mountains. The clouds were moving fast towards us and the wind was whipping up. The sky looked like a huge gray monster with cloud fangs.

The blizzard began, and within a few minutes it was leaving enough on the road that you could see the car's tire tracks in front of us.

As we got out near to my country neighborhood, the branches in the trees, now barren of their leaves, were blowing around, looking like giant skeleton arms.

I was watching one of the girls in the front seat. She never talks to me on the way to school or home from school either. She is the one who picks her nose and eats it. That totally grosses me out, on account of her Mom always saying things like: "Gabriel, isn't Angie just the prettiest little thing in her new dress and matching hair bows? I mean she could be a model, this cutie of mine."

Angie sometimes acts embarrassed and says, "Mmmm-o-mmmm, cut it out!" Other times she just beams and runs her snotty fingers through her hair.

 I wonder if her mom would think her Angie was such a princess if she caught her with her finger all the way up her schnoz. I hope she hits the brakes really hard sometime, and Angie's finger goes all the way inside her big, blond head. I also think she should send Angie with an extra sandwich to school if she is hungry enough to eat her own boogers, YUCK!

I feel like shoving my finger all the way down my throat, and I want to make really big gagging noises, but that would be rude, so I just look at her with a blank face.

The windshield wipers were slapping extra hard through the snow, and the car was slipping around. It was pretty cool to ride in a swerving car, reminding me of the toboggan rides we take down the big hill, but Mrs. Abernathy didn't seem to be enjoying it. Her knuckles on both hands were totally white as she gripped the steering wheel.

Instead of dropping me off two blocks from my house like she always did, Mrs. Abernathy dropped me right in front of my house and told me to hurry in. What did she think I was made of, sugar? Just because her goofy daughters had hair that would wilt in the snow didn't mean everyone should stay out of it. As I got out of her car, I thanked her, wished her a great weekend, stuck my tongue out at her daughters when they weren't looking and started to stick my tongue out to catch some delicious snow flakes.

When I got in the house, Dad was already home from work.

"Hello, young man! How was your day?"

"Fine. How was your day, Dad?"

"Simply grand," he grinned. "I let my afternoon classes out early and came home to get ready for the big one. We may lose electricity, so I have collected enough candles to start a royal bonfire, and we have enough food and water to last us a century!"

Mom walked in laughing. She patted Dad on the arm and said, "I don't know who the bigger boy is, you or Gabe!"

She gave Dad a peck on the cheek, and he grabbed her and bent her backwards, dipping her low and smooching her right on the lips the way you see people do when they are doing that fancy dancing stuff in the old black and white movies.

"Dad, cut it out, that is so yuck!"

Dad started making more disgusting lip-smacking noises.

Dad brought Mom back upright, and they were both laughing. My dad was in the best mood ever!

"How are you, darling?" Mom turned to me and gave me a hug.

"I'm great, Mom! Can I go out and play in the snow?"

"Sure, just be home in time for dinner! Put on those warm wool socks I just got you, and make sure to wear the heavier gloves. It is colder than you think."

"Okay, Mom!" I sprinted up the stairs to my room to get my socks, a turtleneck sweater, and another sweatshirt to wear over it.

I ran back down to the kitchen and grabbed the phone to call Andy.

"Hello, Mrs. Epstein, may I please speak to Andy?"

Andy's mom called about three names before she got his right: "Johnny, Ritch..., Teddy, Jer..., doggone it, I mean ANDY! GABRIEL'S ON THE TELEPHONE FOR YOU!!"

Andy's mom was always doing that. She would go through

all four brother's names before she got the one she wanted. I guess when you have that many kids it's hard to keep them all straight, though sometimes Mom does that to me and she only has two.

It took forever for Andy to come to the phone.

"H-H-Hello?"

"Why do you answer the phone like you don't know it's me? I heard your mom tell you it was me!"

"I w-w-was in the b-bathroom, t-turdbrain. I d-didn't hear her. Wh-What's up?"

"Meet me down at the lake! Call Butch!"

Andy said he would call Butch, and so within the next fifteen minutes the Brotherhood would assemble because Butch would call Tony and Tony would call Craig and Craig wouldn't call Murph.

"Where you going, chicken-butt?" Carl snarled at me as he sat on the floor by the front door pulling his boots on.

"CARL, GO TO YOUR ROOM! I TOLD YOU TO STOP CALLING

"MOO-OOM, come on! I was just kidding around!"

"I don't care! Go to your room and see if you can think long and hard about not doing that again." Mom was doing the hand-on the-hips thing, which meant she was really serious.

"But Mom..."

"I don't want to hear your 'buts'... just go!"

Dad chimed in, "Carl, you heard your mom, now GO!"

Dad gave Carl 'the look,' the one that meant business and you didn't argue with.

"FINE! Why do I have to have such a lame-o for a brother?"

Carl pulled his boot off, threw it into the closet, stomped up the stairs and slammed his door.

"Uh oh." I thought. If there was one thing dad didn't like, it was slamming doors.

Dad headed up the stairs and I headed out of the house as fast as I could to avoid the mid-winter fireworks.

CHAPTER THIRTEEN

Under The Ice

When I got down to the lake, one by one my buddies showed up. We skated around on our shoes in a quick pickup game of hockey, using a rock and some sticks that we left near the dock for just these occasions. Snow was falling and a cold wind was whipping down the canyon across the ice, dropping the temperature fast. Everyone's breath was coming out in big white clouds.

We were shouting and pushing each other down in the snow, just having a great old time. When it started to get dark, Mr. Patchett yelled from his back patio, "You boys get off that ice now. Get on home before it's too late, before the ghost Indian breaks up through the ice and pulls the bunch of you down under for all that dadgum racket you're making!"

Craig yelped, "Oh man, I was supposed to be home a long time ago!" and dashed off the ice.

"CHICKEN!" two of us yelled.

"Whatever!" Craig yelled, disappearing near the sandstone cliffs.

Just hearing Mr. Patchett mention the ghost Indian again made my skin crawl, and I could tell the other guys felt so too. "I, uh, better get going. Dinner is probably already on the table..."

"Man, Mr. Patchett's weird!" Butch snarled, heading as fast as he could off the ice. "Ghost Indian, what a joke!"

But Butch looked a bit more worried than he was letting on.

"I heeeaaardd you...."

Mr. Patchett's voice carried with the wind. It sounded eerie, and made us all walk just a bit faster across the ice toward home.

Andy whispered, "Yeah, he thinks w-w-we believe all of his r-ridiculous stories, b-b-but I don't, do you, G-Gabe?"

I looked at Andy and knew by the look in his eye that he just wasn't sure what to think and neither was I, but neither one of us was going to hang around to find out.

"Nah, come on, Andy, Mr. Patchett is just a crazy old guy, and he is always going on and on about the ghost Indian."

"B-But he lives r-right here. W-Wouldn't he know b-better than anyone?" Andy's face looked like he had seen a ghost already.

With my foot, I cleared a space on the ice below my feet and looked down. It was murky, but I thought I saw an eye looking back at me through about a foot of thick ice. Shivers ran up my spine and I took off running.

"AGHHH, YOU GUYS, SOMETHING IS DOWN THERE!"

All of a sudden, everyone was slipping around, trying to get their footing and trying to get off of the ice as fast as possible.

"Come on Peters, you didn't really see anything... did you?" Tony shivered, scooting off the ice.

"Heeeeee's going to geeeeet youuuuuuuuuuuuuuuu...."

When I got to my house I ran in and slammed the door behind me. At first I stood there panting like my dogs, who met me at the door, but both of them started snarling and barking at something unseen on the other side of the door, which sent a huge shiver up my spine.

Evil eye under the ice
Is watching over me
I think I'll stay away from the lake
Is it real? Could it really be?

It took me about two seconds to clear the stairs and get under the covers in the upper bunk. When I finally felt brave enough, I parted the curtains and looked outside. About a block away, I saw a huge figure disappearing beyond the light coming from the streetlight in the cold, black night. I could have sworn he was wearing tan buckskin clothes.

I pulled out my binoculars to try to see what was out there better. Under the streetlight I could make out what looked like footprints or, more specifically, moccasin prints.

Just then the phone rang, startling me as much as if someone screamed in my ear. I had a phone in my room now, so I picked it up, fully thinking the voice on the other end would be the ghost Indian. "Hullo?" I whispered hoarsely.

"Gabe?" Andy whispered, "D-Did you r-really s-see eyes in the ice?"

"Yeah, I really did. It was the spookiest thing I have seen in a long time."

"S-Seriously, c-come on, T-T-Tell me the t-truth!"

"Cross my heart on the Secret Brotherhood, Andy."

"Oh my gosh, I'm n-never going back d-down there again!"

Now that I was home in my bunkbeds, I started to calm down a little and my more logical side started to work, making me doubt the whole Indian legend thing

"Come on, Andy, we've been there a million times, and no ghost Indian has ever nabbed any of us."

We talked about it for a while, and then decided that the eyeball I had seen was probably more likely that of the ghost carp than the ghost Indian that Mr. Patchett always talks about. I went along with that idea since Andy suggested it, and he seemed to really want it to be a fish, not a ghost Indian who would come through the ice at any moment, or worse yet, when we were out on the boat fishing come spring. The more we talked about it, the more confused I felt.

After I hung up the phone, I still felt pretty uneasy so I crept across the hall to Carl's room. The light was on, and I could hear heavy breathing coming from his room like he was wrestling or something. I wondered what he was doing in there.

When I cracked the door open enough to see him, I saw that he was lying on his back on his bed with the book Where The Red Fern Grows* lying across his face, and he was snorting and snoring. Curled up next to him was both Friskier and Flop. My dog, my cat, and my book were all taking a nap with my brother.

I sneaked back into my room and got up on the upper bunk and peeked out the window into the dark night, hoping to catch a view of the ghost Indian and yet not wanting to at the same time.

After dinner Dad walked around with his transistor radio hooked to his belt so he could listen in on two of his favorite weather channels. Voices crackled on and on about the storm and what was happening in the surrounding states.

Dad gave us minute-by-minute updates in his best weathercaster voice: "The storm is moving from the Pacific West coast, marching eastward and dumping rain in the lower states. By the time it gets to Utah and Colorado it is pounding snow."

My dad would basically say the same thing the person on his radio had just said, even though we all could hear it.

"That's nice, dear," Mom would say over and over, and then give Carl and me a look or roll her eyes and smile.

She whispered and motioned to the book she was reading, "I have read the same sentence five times now...."

I smiled back at Mom and then asked Dad, "So, Dad is a storm coming?"

Dad gave me a curious look and then we all burst out laughing.

Dad then said, "There's also a storm sweeping down from Canada, and one coming up from Mexico carrying millions of gal-

*Where The Red Fern Grows is a book written by Wilson Rawls.

lons of ocean water and planning to converge right over our house in Colorado."

"Really, Dad, where'd you hear that?" Carl asked, motioning his head toward the radio on Dad's belt.

"I, uh..."

We all broke out laughing again since dad was just repeating what the radio kept reporting over and over.

Dad just shook his head and headed downstairs to bring up more wood for the fireplace.

I could hear Dad out in the garage talking to himself, "THIS IS GOING TO BE A DOOZY TO END ALL DOOZIES! THE SKI RESORTS WILL LIVE ON THIS STORM FOR YEARS TO COME! WE BETTER BATTEN DOWN THE HATCHES! HUNKER DOWN FOR A TRUE, EASTERN-STYLE STORM!"

CHAPTER FOURTEEN

Blizzard

The next morning, I looked out my bedroom window, and about a foot of snow had piled up next to the window on the roof. The wind was blowing the snow hard and making giant drifts in the field across the street. The sky was really dark and looked like it was so low you would scrape your head on it.

Dad must have kept piling the wood on the hearth after I went to bed. He'd put an entire forest within reach of the fireplace.

Mom kept making comments about how Dad was like a little boy on the first day of summer, or in my dad's case, the first day of winter. Dad's a weather nut!; he loves lighting storms, blizzards and huge rainstorms. My dad is the only grownup you will ever see in the summer, when we get a huge rainstorm, running up and down the gutters and collecting long night crawlers from the street to put in his garden.

There is this weather guy on the television with plastic hair and a deep voice called Scooter Anderson, so sometimes Mom calls Dad Scooteranderson (all one word, the way she says it) because of how much he talks about the weather.

It snowed all day Saturday too, and accumulated about two and a half feet in the yard, but then suddenly stopped. I thought my dad was going to be heartbroken.

But his transistor radio told him and us that we had only seen the beginning of what we could expect, so instantly his spirits lifted, and he went to the garage to split more wood.

On Sunday, during the day, it snowed again, but not as hard as we might have hoped to assure some snow days off of school. But on Sunday night the bulk of the storm we had been hearing so much about crept over the mountains and began to move over the foothills near where we live. Just as it was getting dark, it started to snow like you would imagine at the North Pole. It looked like the clouds had moved in just over the roofs of the houses in my neighborhood and weren't planning on going anywhere soon. My dad calls the kind of snow that was coming down 'bird feathers,' on account of the fact that they flutter in big, tasty flakes - not that bird feathers would be tasty, but cause these kind of snowflakes coat your whole tongue.

Dad grew up near the ocean on the east coast in upper New York, and their weather in the winter is brutal: "We don't even know what snow is like here. You want to know about a storm? Well, one time..."

My dad would launch into story after story about blizzards sweeping down over their farm, paralyzing the whole county for weeks. There were ice storms* that killed people just standing below their roofs, where ten feet of snow would avalanche down, catching them in mid-sentence, only to be dug out later as solid blocks of ice. Occasionally, a killer icicle would come down and slice someone clean in half.

He would go on and on about storms so huge that the snow would build up against a house and choke the very oxygen out of

*ice storm (noun), a storm of freezing rain that leaves a coating of ice.

the house. His storm stories were his favorites. He could go on for days, and I always wondered why, if he loved deep snow and huge rainstorms so much, we didn't live in upstate New York, where so many of our relatives still lived.

The bird-feather snow kept falling and falling, all through dinner and then all through the evening. The television was on, and the news guy kept breaking into the program to tell us that we were about to get the biggest snowstorm Colorado had gotten since maybe the turn of the century. Wow, that's a long time.

Scooteranderson was telling us that by morning it would turn into a full-scale blizzard with low patterns and upslope, blah, blah, blah. But the only thing I was waiting to hear was that school was canceled!

Our phone was ringing off the hook, with our friends calling to see if we had heard anything yet. We were all planning to spend the next day down on the lake playing hockey, sledding, ice fishing and building snow forts and having snowball wars and building snowmen armies and... we were all so excited about the thought of having a day off of school that we could hardly stand it. We agreed that the first one to hear that school was officially canceled was supposed to let everyone else know. The only problem for me was that I went to a different school than all the other guys, but I knew if it was bad enough to close down the public school, mom wouldn't make me go to St. Joe's.

I went to my closet and dug out every stitch of warm wool socks, gloves, coats, long john underwear and boots. I was going to have twenty changes of clothes ready, so all I would have to do when I got soaking wet was run into the garage and into the basement where I would have my clothes lined up, so I could get changed and be back out in the snow fast and no one would know I had left.

It took me about an hour to find my ice skates since there is a big pile of junk in my closet. Plus, Flop wouldn't move off of the heater vent. He was on it so long that my room was starting to feel like a an icebox.

"Come on, Flopster, I'll cover you up."

I lifted him up onto the upper bunk and petted him hard like he likes. He started to purr like a mini bike engine. His eyes were getting tired and his eyelids were closing. All of a sudden he fell dead asleep and fell to the floor, FLOP!

You could hear Flopster hit the floor from every room in the house. It happened so often that we didn't really even notice anymore, and besides there were pillows below the high places just for him, so he'd have a soft landing. Having a cat with narcolepsy is a total crack up.

I went back to my closet, and as I was throwing things out, Mom came in and said how delighted she was that I was cleaning my room. She came back in with a dust cloth, the vacuum and all the other stuff it would take to really clean my room really good. Carl threw me a really dirty look from across the hall when Mom told him she wanted him to do the same thing.

At the bottom of my closet in the corner that I hadn't seen for I don't know how long, I found something that made me sad. Stimey was stuck to the wall. Stimey was my frog. He had lived in a fish tank in my closet for a month right next to my guinea pigs Squeaky and Squeakier and then just disappeared into thin air, or so I had thought. I always somehow figured Stimey had found his way down the stairs, out the back door and into the ditch behind our house. Now I found out Stimey had gotten out of his fish tank and tried to find a way out through my mess. He had gotten wedged right up against the wall, and now was as stiff and skinny as a board. He smelled kind of rank-sweet, and had a funny look on his face like when my granny yawns.

It would be a while before I could bury Stimey in the back yard on account of the frozen ground, so I pushed him into the back of my sock drawer, right next to a cool rattlesnake skin I had found and three huge stink beetle bugs that were in a jar getting crispy. They were supposed to have been for a stink bomb that I was going to put in Carl's room.

You take a baby food jar and poke holes in the lid and leave just enough grass and junk for the stink beetle bugs to live on for weeks. Hide it really well because when the stink beetle bugs realize they aren't going anywhere and that they are stuck in there with other bugs they get really mad and start lifting their bottoms and let go the worst smell you have ever smelled. It is so bad that it makes a dog sneeze if they are ever dumb and curious enough to sniff a stink beetle walking across the concrete.

ANYWAY, I never got to drill the holes in the lid and the three stink beetle bugs must have died from lack of air. I bet if I opened the jar you could smell them all the way to Andy's house.

Maybe I would use them after all in Carl's room. I could just open the jar and leave them hanging in a pocket of one of Carl's pants in his closet. It would be months before he figured out where the bad smell was coming from, and Mom would be on his case every day to find the source of the stink, heh heh.

The snowflakes started to get smaller and fall about twice as fast. My dad started filling every jug, pitcher, cooking pot, and glass we owned with water and lining them up on the kitchen counter. I was glad he was doing that because last year we had a big storm that knocked out our electricity and water for a day, and Dad started taking the water out of the back of the toilets.

"Oh come on, it is fresh water just like any other water in the house." Dad explained.

But from the toilet? I mean, I would rather die of thirst than drink toilet water!

I started thinking about how it would be really fun to hang out in the tree house during the entire blizzard, but you would need like ten thousand blankets and sleeping bags or you would freeze to death. It would definitely be my place to hide during the snowball war. It was a perfect place with hidey-holes that you could duck in and out of, and the walls kept you from getting clobbered, plus it was a lot harder to throw a snowball up into a tree than to throw one down from one. Andy and I would haul bucket after bucket of snow up into the tree house to make snowballs out of, and we would whup on our big brothers!

Later on Mom came into my room to "tuck me in." Even though I am a big boy now and don't really need Mom to tuck me in, I really like it when she does. She usually sings a song in my ear, reads a bit of a book with me or asks me to tell her a story that I have imagined from a real event in the day and then she always kisses my forehead and tells me how happy she is to have me. I get such a warm and cozy feeling when Mom does that, that it's almost embarrassing to describe it.

Tonight I hugged Mom's neck extra hard. Dad ducked his head in my door and told me goodnight and that he loved me.

Mom tucked Carl in too, and I could hear the low murmur of my dad's radio coming up the stairs as he kept track of the storm.

In the dark of my bedroom I felt so excited, I could hardly stand it. The room felt cold, but I was snuggly in my blanket and the snow piling up against the house made me feel lucky to be in my warm bed. I looked out the window and could barely make out the street light across the street, but it looked like a large figure was there staring at my house. I ducked down hard and kept peeking out the window. The snow got in the way, so I couldn't really tell if someone was out there or not.

I thought of the times I had told my big brother scary stories about this wild monster guy who was in our neighborhood. Carl would then sneak out of our room when he thought I was asleep and go sleep in Mom and Dad's room or in the bathtub. I started thinking that might not be such a bad idea, and then wished for a moment that I still shared a bedroom with my idiot big brother.

For the first time in my life, I went and cracked my door open and turned on the hall light and then jumped into the lower bunk and pulled the covers around me.

"Frisky, come on boy," I called.

His tail started thumping the ground.

"Come on, boy!"

He got up and came to the edge of my bed and put his nose on the mattress. I could see his big brown eyes looking up at me. I kissed his head and pulled him up onto my bed and curled up next to him real close. Frisky would never let any dumb ghost Indian get near me, even though I knew there was no such thing.

Pretty soon Friskier got curious and came over and jumped up on the bed too. Either the bed was getting smaller or I was growing, because the three of us were a little too much for the bed anymore. Someone turned off the hall light, probably thinking that

Carl or I had forgotten it after a trip to the bathroom since we never needed the hall light anymore, but I figured that was okay; my dogs were protecting me now I could look up through the bottom of the drawn curtains and see that the snow was coming straight down one minute and then sideways the next. The wind was howling, the roof right below my window was piling up with snow, and the snow edging toward the window closed off my view from the bottom bunk. By morning my window might disappear in a snowdrift.

Downstairs Mom had some Christmas music playing on her record player, and I could see the reflection of the fire in the fireplace on the hall wall, making the wall seem to move like the reflection of orange water.

It seemed to warm the whole house when the fireplace was blazing, and the scent of pine from the wood stacked on the hearth and the fresh Christmas tree made the whole house smell delicious, like Christmas itself.

Every so often Carl or I would call out from his room that the snow was coming faster and the blizzard was really beginning. "YAHOOOO!" Dad yelled, and then you could hear my mom giggling and telling him to keep it down because we were trying to sleep.

It was going to be hard to sleep with the big storm.

My mom called up, "You boys go to sleep now. You just might have to go to school tomorrow, and I don't want to send walking zombies off to school!"

Carl and I groaned loudly at the very thought that my mother would say the word 'school' on such a night as this, but soon I was fast asleep dreaming of shadowy figures out there in the snow, and then I started dreaming about the ghost Indian from the lake who was climbing up the patio toward my bedroom window.

I awakened to the loud sound of a tree branch popping against the house as it bent in the wind. The cars parked on the street looked like they had grown twice as tall, and the trees looked full against the night sky - like they did in the summer when they were full of leaves. I was watching all of this from my upper bunk, and it was about midnight. Frisky and Friskier had gotten too hot and were back down on the floor, so I moved up to the upper bunk where Flop was next to me now.

Flopster was purring like a mini bike engine, as usual. He was so happy that he had a place to curl up on my warm bunk with me.

Frisky was sleeping soundly in his favorite corner, but Friskier was acting kind of weird. She kept pacing back and forth from my bed to Carl's door. I thought it was so weird that I flipped my body down into the lower bunk again and started to stroke her silky fur.

"What's the matter, girl?"

She looked at me like she was just about to talk. I swear sometimes she can, but she doesn't want to give up her secret.

She got up and walked over to Carl's door and sat, one paw on the bottom of the door. I heard Carl in his room groaning.

I pushed the door open. "Carl?"

"Oh, my head hurts," he sniffled loudly, and then let out a couple deep-sounding coughs.

"Are you okay?" I flipped his light on.

His face was beet red, and his eyes looked totally glazed over.

"Carl, what's wrong?"

"I can't lift my head. It feels like I have I have cotton stuffed in between my ears... they hurt sooooo bad.... Can you get Mom?"

He sounded so pathetic. I felt bad for him. He hadn't even called me a bad name.

I pushed Mom and Dad's door open. Dad was snoring, but there was a smile on his face. I imagined that the storm that was raging outside was inside his head too. "Mom," I whispered, and touched her arm.

She sprang up.

"Gabe, is everything okay?"

"Something's wrong with Carl."

She pulled her robe around her shoulders and followed me to his room. Carl was groaning and Friskier had her nose on his bed right next to his face.

"Carl, what's the matter, honey?"

Something happened that I almost never see. Carl had tears streaming down the sides of his face.

"Mom, my ear hurts so bad. My head, too." Mom put her hand on Carl's forehead and then she pressed her forehead to his. "Oh honey, you have a fever. Gabe, please go get the thermometer and the orange aspirin out of the hall closet."

It was called 'baby aspirin,' but she knew Carl and I wouldn't take it if she called it that). She then started to ask Carl all kinds of questions. I brought the thermometer and aspirin back to Mom, and then she told me to go back to bed.

I sat up on my upper bunk for a long time watching the blizzard, and right before I fell back asleep I said a little prayer for Carl to be okay.

When I woke up in the morning the sky was still gray and snow was coming down even harder than it had been in the middle of the night. The snow had blown up against the front of the house and covered half of my window. Dad must have heard me up and moving around, because he stuck his smiling face into my room.

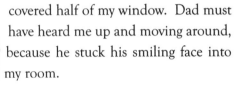

"Gabe, school's canceled! It's a snow day, nothing to do but play in the snow and have fun!"

"Are you going to work today, Dad?"

"Can't, my young man, the roads are closed!"

"WOW, COOL!" I shouted.

"Shhhh... Carl is still in bed. He is a sick puppy."

"What a bummer," I whispered. "Sick on a snow day?"

"Yeah, but we'll get him on his feet in no time."

CHAPTER FIFTEEN
Mr. Epstein

Not too many adults came out of their houses the first day of the snowstorm. The streets were crawling with kids though, throwing snowballs, pulling sleds and everything else you could imagine.

Down and up the street you could hear shovels scraping through the snow and muffled voices of play. The snow made everything sound so quiet.

For the first time in a long time I went into Andy's house to warm up. Andy ran up stairs, "I HAVE TO G-GO TO THE B-B-BATHROOM. I'LL MEET YOU IN THE K-K-KITCHEN, G-GABE!"

"OKAY!" My fingers were tingling from the cold.

When I walked into the kitchen it felt like a million spiders crawled up the back of my back. Andy's dad was sitting at the kitchen table sipping on something that was steaming.

"Hello, Gabriel."

I hadn't seen him close up since last summer as I had been avoiding Andy's house since the big blow up.

"Hello, Mr. Epstein. How are you feeling?" I wanted to take back that last sentence the minute it came out of my mouth.

"I feel fine. How do you feel?"

"Uh, I, uh, I'm a little cold."

I felt so stupid for asking him how he was feeling. Maybe I wasn't even supposed to know about his problem and Andy would get in trouble for telling me.

"Would you like some hot chocolate?"

Mr. Epstein stood up and went to the stove. I had forgotten how tall he was. His bright red head looked like it was going to hit the ceiling. He and Andy both had the electric red hair in the family.

He turned around, smiling, and handed me a steaming mug of hot chocolate. Then he grabbed a can of whipped cream on the counter and made a big cone on top of my mug. "Sit."

I sat like his Afghan* dogs do when Mr. Epstein commands them.

"So... what's new, Gabriel?"

I felt really nervous, and wished someone else would come in right then. "What's new, hmmm, let me see... The snowstorm is new. What's new with you?"

"Um, not much really." Mr. Epstein smiled and looked right into my eyes. "Your leg looks like it is all better now."

"Yeah, I think they are about the same length now. I don't hobble much anymore."

It felt weird to be talking to Andy's dad like this. Usually he had seemed kind of mean and I didn't like to be around him.

"Well, that's good. Good to see things can improve, eh... Yup, things are looking up all around."

Mr. Epstein leaned forward and patted the top of my hand.

I didn't know if he was talking about things looking up for him or me, but he was being really nice. I couldn't remember one time when Mr. Epstein had talked to me or been this nice to me. The weird thing was, he reminded me of Andy, and Andy is one of the best guys I know!

Andy came bounding down the stairs and stood there in the kitchen door, kind of out of breath. "Hey D-Dad, wh-what's up?"

Andy's dad gave him a quick hug, "Hey Andy, you guys going skating?"

"Probably, the other g-guys are m-m-meeting us d-down there

*Afghan - short for Afghan hound

and..."

"Would you mind if I came down there? My old hockey skates are resurfaced, and I thought I might give them a try."

"Seriously? Th-That would be AWESOME, D-Dad! When?"

Andy looked like he was going to burst. I knew it was because he hadn't done anything with his dad for a long time, but I kind of thought Andy might be relieved too on account of the ghost Indian and all.

Andy's dad sat back at the table. "You tell me. You sure I wouldn't be intruding on your fun?"

Andy walked over and put his arm around his dad's shoulder. He whispered something in his dad's ear. Andy's dad looked like he was going to cry. I just looked at the pattern of wood swirls on the table and chugged down the rest of my hot chocolate.

"Okay, I'll come down there and skate a bit. It's been a long time."

"Sure, D-D-Dad, that'd be g-g-great!"

"Hey, what would you two guys think of me taking you all camping next spring? Maybe your dad would want to come along, Gabriel? Maybe your whole gang, what is it, the Secret something or other?"

"YEAH!" Andy and I both said at the same time. Andy looked happier than I had ever seen him.

"Could we g-go to the l-lake? We could w-water ski like we used to."

Andy's dad nodded with a faraway look in his eyes.

Andy started pulling on tons of clothes with the biggest smile on his face.

"I'll meet you guys down at the lake in about half an hour, okay?"

Andy's dad stood up again. He towered over both of us, and Andy was pretty tall.

Andy pulled his coat on and his gloves. "That'll be so g-g-great!"

His dad hugged him again, this time picking him up off his feet.

I just fiddled with a button on the stove, not sure what to say.

Andy and I headed back out into the blowing wind and hopped through the snow. Every so often one of us would tackle the other and we would roll around making snow angels and practice our wrestling moves. I thought the smile on Andy's face was going to freeze on permanently.

There was so much snow on the lake that it took us half an hour to clear off the ice to play hockey and skate. We had teams and were skating around when Andy's dad showed up with two of Andy's older brothers. The three of them were so tall, they looked like real hockey players. Andy's dad moved around the ice like no one else could.

"WOW, I am rusty!" he yelled when he passed us faster than anyone else had ever skated on the ice.

"Wow, if that is rusty, I'd like to see when he's practiced up," Butch yelled.

Andy just grinned from ear to ear and so did his big brothers.

Then the Epsteins were all out on the ice, "Come on, it's us against all of you!" Andy's older brother Teddy snarled.

Even though they were outnumbered three to one, it was sure they would win.

Then Andy's dad said, "The Epsteins and Gabe, that is!" Andy tugged me across the ice to join all of them.

We glided up and down the lake, slapping shots into the other team's goals. Butch and Tony kept trying to skate me into the rocks, and I just laughed and joined one of Andy's brothers who protected me as I handled the puck.

Andy's dad showed us all his slap shot and some other really cool moves from his "glory days."

Jeremy and Teddy, Andy's brothers, yelled, "GO DAD! Kill it! WOOOOHOOOOO!"

Andy's dad just glided around the ice handling the puck like a professional. Everyone else was in awe. No one had known Andy's dad was so cool.

After about half an hour of hockey Andy's dad went over and sat down on some rocks. "Man, my old ankles are killing me!" he complained. He peeled off his sock and held his feet up to show us all his blisters. Andy skated over to him and did a kill stop, spraying him with snow and ice. They both were laughing, and I felt so good for my best friend.

When Andy's dad left the lake everyone was talking about how cool he was and how they each wished they could skate like him. Andy and his brothers just stood there beaming, then Teddy and Jeremy started jogging to catch up with their dad. Teddy turned and yelled, "YO, GABE, YOU DID GREAT!"

"THANKS, JEREMY, YOU DID, TOO!"

I thought about how goofy my response was. Of course he did great - he was two times everyone's size on the ice. But it felt good to have someone think it was cool that I was on his team after all I had been through with my bad leg and all.

The wind was extra cold, so we didn't stay down at the lake too much longer. After a few hours we all went to our houses for lunch, and then Andy, Tony and Butch came down to my house to play monopoly and drink hot chocolate and eat Mom's famous chocolate peanut butter popcorn**.

It snowed all day and the rest of the night. Tony got to spend the night, which was fun, but I felt kind of bad because Carl didn't even come out of his room the whole night he felt so awful. Still, it was kind of nice for a change to have a friend stay over that my brother didn't torment with rude comments.

** *famous chocolate peanut butter popcorn recipe - pop the popcorn using fresh butter, then add melted chocolate and peanut butter, drizzled over the popcorn. Salt lightly and stir well. Add a scary movie or two, and plenty of red cream soda!*

CHAPTER SIXTEEN

Tragedy In A Snowstorm!

The next morning Mom told Carl she thought he had an ear infection and a really bad cold. He would have to wrap up really well and wear a hat if and when he got to go outside.

That afternoon when Mom finally let him go outside, Tony, Carl and I were throwing snow off the driveway into a huge pile where we were going to build our snow fort to challenge the older brothers to a snowball fight when a piercing shriek filled the air. Something big rumbled up the old gravel road from the highway.

In the not-too-far away distance we could hear several sirens coming from the direction of town. We all dropped our shovels and ran to the gravel road to see what was happening. People were standing in their picture windows trying to get a view of what the ruckus was all about.

"Let's go, guys, that's a fire truck siren! That's a police car!"

As we ran down the gravel road and rounded the corner, an ambulance came spinning up the street. Then not far behind a fire truck was spinning its way up the road, and a police car. You could hear the chains on the tires grinding away at the snow, and it was all they could do to get them into our neighborhood. Everyone along the way who was outside dropped his or her shovel to go see what all of the excitement was about.

As we turned the corner on Mars Boulevard, I could see that they had all gathered around Mean Mrs. Rickles' house. I won't tell you what the first thought that came to my mind was. I am really ashamed of myself for it now, because of what happened.

Everyone for blocks around had bundled up and come to see what all the fuss was about. The snow muffled all of the conversations, but the murmuring was loud. After a little while the ambulance lady pushed this wheelie cart thing out to the front porch, where Mr. Rickles was now lying on his back on a stretcher all connected to tubes and stuff. The lady was having a hard time pushing the cart through all of the snow, so neighbors started to push and pull and help her get the cart to the ambulance.

Ryan Rickles and his mom, Mean Mrs. Rickles stood on the porch. Mean Mrs. Rickles had her hand over her mouth, and her eyes were wider than I have ever seen anyone open them. She looked like she was totally afraid of something, and the ghost Indian flashed through my mind. Mean Mrs. Rickles' body was moving like she was crying really hard and trying to hide it.

Ryan wasn't hiding anything; he just kept screaming, "DADDY? Mommy, is Daddy going to be okay? Mommy, tell me..."

They were both crying now, and that gave me a really sick feeling. All of a sudden Mean Mrs. Rickles just kind of collapsed into the snow. She fell face down on her knees, crying hard.

It felt like the dark sky had filled my whole head. A couple of the moms took Ryan into the house I guess, so he wouldn't have to see his mom so sad.

Grandma Peroni, who lives next door to Mean Mrs. Rickles, walked up onto the Rickles porch and lifted Mean Mrs. Rickles up out of the snow and held her in her arms. Gadfly

Peroni's grandma is so big that Mean Mrs. Rickles just about disappeared.

It was weird. The snow kept falling hard, and the quiet that I usually like about winter and storms now felt really eerie. The tension in the air was so thick it felt like something big was just about to explode. The wind was blowing, and this high-pitched eerie moaning sound filled the street suddenly as they closed the ambulance door. It gave me the shivers.

The ambulance and fire truck started their sirens and moved down Mars Boulevard behind the police car, headed toward town and the hospital. A bunch of our neighbors gathered in the street and were talking about what had just happened, trying to guess what it was all about, but no one wanted to ask her.

Poor Ryan was now kneeling on the couch inside with his hands pressed against the window, and a couple of the moms were trying to help him while his mom was outside watching the ambulance turn the corner.

All of my buddies stood there with their mouths hanging open. They couldn't believe their eyes. Kids huddled close to their parents, and even my brother came over and put his huge arm around my shoulder. What was weird was somehow I knew my brother wasn't really doing that to comfort me, but to help himself.

Then Dad came jogging down the street. He stopped and talked to Mr. Morris for a minute, and then came over to where Carl and I were standing.

"Let's go home, boys."

Dad walked over to Mean Mrs. Rickles and Gadfly's grandma and said something to Mean Mrs. Rickles. She nodded and then Dad walked home with us in total silence. I could tell Dad wanted to say something, but just didn't know what to say. I know how that feels, so I didn't say anything either.

When we got home, I went to my bedroom and sat on the floor with my dogs. I played with Legos, and thought about calling Andy just to talk, but somehow I fell asleep and didn't wake up until mom knocked on my door with a plate of cookies and a mug of peppermint hot chocolate.

Later, Dad called Carl and me downstairs to join him and Mom. He had been on the phone with Mr. Morris. We all sat at the kitchen table except for Dad, who was pacing back and forth. Both Mom and Dad looked serious, and I could tell they were going to tell us something bad.

"What's up, Dad?" Carl asked.

"Mr. Rickles died." It just came out that matter-of-fact.

"WHAT?" Carl and I said together.

Mom's eyes were filled with tears, "What are they going to do? He was young. Oh my gosh, I have to do something."

Mom started pulling pots and pans out of the cupboards.

"Lasagna or spaghetti? Which should I make for them?" But she wasn't really asking anybody.

"Wow, that is lousy," Carl muttered.

I thought about what I had been thinking when I first saw the ambulance at Mean Mrs. Rickles' house, and it made me feel really bad now. I hadn't wished anything bad on Mr. Rickles or anything, but I had thought of something bad for her. Now I felt lousy. No matter how mean she was, no one should have to lose her husband and the father of her son.

Mom got on the phone with the other moms in the neighborhood, and pretty soon lasagna and spaghetti and casseroles were being organized for the Rickles.

That night as I pulled the covers up to my ears I started to feel really, really scared. If Ryan Rickles' dad could have a heart attack and he was the same age as my dad, my dad might, too. Just thinking about it made my stomach hurt. I felt really bad for Ryan, and decided I was going to do something nice for him even though I didn't really like him.

I slipped out of my bed and tiptoed down the hall. Dad was sitting in his easy chair reading a book while Mom was puttering around in the kitchen. I walked up and put my arms around Dad's neck. He pulled me onto his lap and we sat there rocking for a little while. Neither one of us said anything.

Even though I felt like I was a little old to be rocking with dad, I liked it a lot. The next morning I woke up in my own bed. Dad had carried me up the stairs and I didn't even wake up.

CHAPTER SEVENTEEN

Ho! Ho! Ho!

Just three more days and we are on Christmas break! I can hardly wait to get out of school! All of the walls at school are decorated with snowflakes and snowmen and all kinds of fun Christmas stuff. Each grade had a contest to see who could make the most creative poster to celebrate Christmas, and one thing for sure is that I didn't win, didn't come close. The thing is that no matter how lousy you draw or paint, you still have to make a poster - it is for an art grade - so I tried something simple and it still turned out lousy. I am using the word 'lousy' because it is a word Charlie Brown uses, usually to describe himself, and I kind of think I am a lot like him sometimes.

The whole school is going to watch Charlie Brown's Christmas in an all-school assembly, which is kind of scary since my school goes from kindergarten to twelfth grade. The big kids always make a bunch of noise, so no one can even hear the movie.

It makes me feel really small to be in with all those big kids, even though most of them seem nice anyway. Mostly they just ignore us younger kids, but some of them treat me kind of special because I look like that T.V. guy Eddie, though that has kind of calmed down quite a bit.

My class is having a party. I am bringing snowman popcorn

ball treats, which took Mom and me about a hundred hours to make. The cool thing about them is that everyone gets three mini popcorn balls, and I used candy corn for the nose leftover from Halloween and some Red Hots for the buttons.

Dad was watching us making fifteen snowmen and thirteen snow women, and commented that it would have been easier to give everyone a popcorn snowball, which I thought was really funny because it wouldn't have to be decorated and all, it would just be popcorn balls, which I already took for the Halloween party.

Dad also grabbed a couple candy corn and popped them into his mouth, "You could just rub them in cocoa and put a few nuts and marshmallows in them to say they're dirty snowballs!" Dad said, chuckling.

That was actually a really good idea, I thought.

"That's not a bad idea, honey, we'll have to remember that one for next year, huh, Gabe?" Mom smiled really big.

I wasn't totally sure she meant it.

Carl came in just as Dad was saying that about the dirty snowballs and said, "Yeah, or Gabe could make lemon snowballs with the snow from the backyard, with a little help from Frisky and Friskier." He started laughing hard at his own dumb joke.

That comment got a chuckle from Dad and a dirty look from Mom.

"Carl, clean it up please."

Mom scowled, but Dad patted him on the back like it wasn't a big deal.

Later Carl was walking by me in the hall and snarled at me.

"Hey, Chicken-weenie, check this one out, I made it up thinking about your sissy little party snowballs! With a lemon I make lemonade, but round the corner fudge is made."

"WHAT?"

I couldn't believe how dense Carl could be. He wasn't even saying the joke right, and what was all the lemon and lemonade talk about anyway? And besides I was taking snowmen and snow-women, not snowballs.

My brother Carl's school hardly does anything about Christmas. I mean, my school goes all out for Christmas, but his has some dumb winter solstice celebration where they all stand in a circle and talk about how much they love all the dirt and stuff!

The thing about going to a Catholic school is that it is all about God and stuff, and with his Son getting His own vacation and all, we have a huge birthday party for Him. We are even allowed to build snowmen and a cool snow fort to hide behind on the front lawn and have snowball fights. Well, at least we were until one of the fifth-grade girls took a snowball right in the face and got a bloody nose that dripped all over the place. I actually saw who did it, but my lips are sealed because if I ever told she would beat me up. The thing that bugged me most was that all the Sisters thought it had to be a boy who did it, but I knew different.

Mother Superior's voice then came over the intercom throughout the whole school. She sounds like God's sister every time.

"STUDENTS, UNTIL FURTHER NOTICE SNOWBALL THROWING OF ANY KIND ARE BANNED ON SCHOOL GROUNDS. THOSE IN VIOLATION WILL BE PUNISHED.

There was a long pause, some nervous giggling and teachers shushing. Then the crackling noise started again.

133

"ALSO, THE BOYS THAT WERE PACKING ICE BALLS WILL BE DISCIPLINED IF THEY ARE FOUND OUT. I WOULD ENCOURAGE ANYONE WHO KNOWS WHO WAS INVOLVED TO COME FORWARD."

Of course I knew the truth.

Then I got this great idea! What if I acted like I felt guilty because I knew who the girl who had thrown the snowball was l, but hadn't told when I was supposed to, and I let her name slip out in my confession on Saturday? The priest, who was sworn to secrecy, wouldn't be sworn to secrecy about the snowball thrower, but about my confession of my guilty conscience. I could find out how good the priests were at telling secrets.

My pathetic candy cane art project is hanging right outside of Mother Superior's office next to a wreath that looks like some professional decorator made it out of green and red pipe cleaners. My poor candy cane is made out of the free construction paper in the art room, and has uneven lines that zigzag instead of cascade down and around like they are supposed to. I ran out of red crayon, so I had to finish the bottom stripe with pink, so it doesn't look too professional at all.

It's kind of embarrassing, so instead of writing my name on the little tag next to it, I wrote my best friend Andy's name, ANDY EPSTEIN, which is kind of funny because he is Jewish, not Catholic and doesn't even celebrate Christmas. No one has noticed, and Andy doesn't even go to my school, but I'm not sure how I am going to get my art grade for it.

All of the teachers are playing Christmas music in their classrooms, moms everywhere helping with the Christmas parties and people are bringing in cookies and Christmas candy to share with everyone. There is a gift exchange, where you have to pick a name out of this box and then you have to buy that person a gift that doesn't cost more than three dollars.

So, I picked this kid named Sam Dudeler. He is a funny kid who always makes this funny face like he has just smelled the worst thing in the world when the teacher says something he doesn't like. It kind of looks like his whole entire face is being pulled up into his eyebrows when he does it, and it cracks me up every time. He wears the same cardigan sweater over his dress shirt every day, which you aren't supposed to do because of our school's dress code, but he gets special permission because he has some weird disease that makes his fingers and toes really cold anytime the temperature drops below one hundred degrees or something like that. He's even poked holes for his thumbs in the end of the sweater so he can cover his hands most of the time. So, I think I will get him some gloves because of his disease. He is always pulling the sleeves of his sweater over his hands in class.

Every year our school has a big Christmas play besides the play about Charlie Brown. It's for the parents to come to in the evening, and the Christmas play is for us kids during the day.

I have to be in the school play now. There was a time when I was so happy and excited about trying out. I thought being in the school play was going to be the absolute greatest thing, but now I dread the thought of it!

I wanted to be in the Charlie Brown play, but didn't get a part after I flubbed my line because I was so nervous because Amy* was sitting right in the front row watching me while she waited to try out. My line was only seven words long, and I practiced it with a totally different voice, just like Linus's voice.

I picked Linus because Sally really likes him, and I heard

*Amy's a cute girl in my class. I, technically don't like girls, but Amy is different. She is really cute and sometimes when she isn't looking I just stare at her. If the guys ever found out, they would tease me so bad, so for now I will keep it a secret. I know if Andy saw her, he would agree with me. She is the prettiest girl in the whole world.

Amy was trying out to be Charlie Brown's little sister Sally. Everyone knew Amy would be Sally if that was what she tried out for because Amy is the most popular girl in fourth grade, and she has the same blond hair as Sally besides.

I was supposed to say, "Hey Charlie Brown, what's in that box?" but instead I said, "Hi Charlie Brown..." My tongue froze and my mind froze; why was Amy looking at me with a scrunched-up face?

Before I could stop my mouth, I finished and flubbed my line with, "Uh, I, Uh, well Charlie Brown, I think your little sister's cute..."

Everyone gasped and looked at Amy. Amy's hand was covering her mouth, and her eyes got really big. All of a sudden the whole place went up with laughter.

Then from the back several guys started saying, "Gabey and Amy sitting in a tree, K I S S I N G...."

My face must have turned ten colors of red as hot as I felt. I jumped off the stage and disappeared down the aisle, but before I did I thought I saw Amy wink at me, or was she blinking out a tear because I had embarrassed her?

So here I was, going to be in the grown-up's Christmas play, which I was dreading. I mean, how can a guy get excited about Christmas when he is the tree in the school play?

I tried out for Joseph...too short, I guess. I tried out for baby Jesus... too old, I guess. I tried out for one of the wise guys... not wise enough, I guess?

I mean, I tried out to be the innkeeper and an angel too, and even a sheep, but the part I got was a tree with these two other nerd-o-rama fourth graders. We all three wear glasses, so it looks totally goofy with our three nerdy faces sticking out of the middle knothole of the trees - three four-eyed geek trees! I look through the middle of the trunk, and you can almost tell it is me from the front row if you can imagine me as a green and brown kid.

The worst part of the whole deal is that Amy is in the play. Of course she is playing the lead role, Mary, and Craig, mister cool guy, mister best athlete, mister foxy-dude, is playing Joseph. So I have to sit there holding up this dumb old tree with my face sticking through, which is ridiculous since there probably weren't any trees in Jesus-land back then.

I don't say anything! I just stand there looking stupid. Technically, I am not even a tree, I am a knot in a tree and I have to stand there watching Craig making googly eyes at Amy, who I think is the prettiest girl I have ever seen in my life.

Hubba-Bubba, Amy is so cute! She doesn't even really even notice me when I am standing right next to her it seems, or maybe she is ignoring me on account of humiliating her at the play tryouts. One time last year she called me a four-eyed geekazoid, and I thought I was going to die. Most people would think it was embarrassing to be called a 'geek' by the one girl they thought was the

cutest girl in the whole wide world, but me? I thought it was super cool that she even noticed me. I mean, think about it, she spent those moments focused just on me, and even though she didn't say the nicest thing, she kind of smiled in a sly way when she said it, like she kind of liked me more than she was letting on. Well anyway, that was what I was hoping was going on.

So Craig gets to hold her hand and help her onto the donkey's back, the donkey being Frank Arenholtz really and not a donkey at all. But I would rather be a donkey carrying Amy... err, Mary, than an old tree any day.

The Christmas party is coming up. I wonder if Amy picked my name and is going to get me some kind of a gift to show me how she really feels about me. At this point, I'm not sure I want to know.

CHAPTER EIGHTEEN

The Monster Jump

During Christmas break, a bunch of the guys got together down in the park above the fishing lake and groomed this great sledding hill with a makeshift bobsled path. We built a bunch of jumps so high that when the inner tube, toboggan or sled hit them we all went flying way down the hill and tumbled all the way to the bottom because of the speed.

We built THE MONSTER, which was the mother of all jumps! THE MONSTER was at least five feet high, and at the top of the jump we built a lip that pushed you back and straight up into the air. Only the bravest of the brave would attempt THE MONSTER solo. A couple of us tested it slow, and it still sent us sky high!

If we could build up a big, fluffy base beneath it, you could land in a huge pile of snow and not get hurt, but right now all the snow that went to build it so high came from the snow below it, so it is D-A-N-G-E-R-O-U-S, with the hardest landing ever! Butch tried it solo and said it was like landing on concrete.

We would have to get back to making a good landing for THE MONSTER, but right now everyone was working on packing the bottom of the hill so you would slide right over the lake and glide for a mile.

Several girls were ice-skating around in figure eights at the other end of the lake. Every so often one of them would yell something at us. For the most part we ignored them, but I noticed Butch was paying pretty close attention to Lisa, and she seemed to be paying attention to him too.

Lisa lived across the street from him, and several times when I went down to his house to see if he wanted to ice fish or something his mom said he was busy. One time I thought it was kind of strange that Butch was inside on a great snowy day, so I sneaked around to his back yard and peeked in the window. He and Lisa were sitting at the table playing some game, and it seemed like he like-liked her, not just that he liked her. He was all weird acting, googly-eyed and laughing at everything she said.

I am starting to think maybe Lisa was Butch's girlfriend and he wasn't telling any of us about it.

Sawyer came down to the lake while we were building it with a pair of skis and boots.

We all laughed at him when he said he was going to go off the THE MONSTER on skis. "You'll kill yourself!" we all agreed.

"No way, you'll never make it!"

"Wait, let me get a camera for this one!" After everyone laughed, Sawyer sulked

"Whatever!" he said and started climbing up the hill.

"Hey,didyouknowthattherewasabattalionofskiersduring theFirstWorldWarfromColoradoand..." Murph was lying on his back on the ice, staring up in the sky.

"SHUT UP, MURPH!" everyone said at the same time.

"GO HOME, WARBOY, AND SHUT UP ABOUT YOUR STUPID BATTLES ALL THE TIME!" Butch snarled.

Murph suddenly sprang to his feet. "YOUSHUTUP,BUTCH!I'MSICKOFYOUTELLINGMEWHAT-TODOALLTHETIME!"

"MAKE ME SHUT UP, WARBOY!" Butch growled, and made a lunging move toward Murph.

All of a sudden Murph leaped onto Butch's back. Butch swung madly at him, and then they were throwing their fists at each other. They landed in the snow and started punching and rolling over and over each other on the lake.

"FIGHT! FIGHT!" all of the boys chanted.

Murph and Butch's arms were flailing, but both had on so many clothes it probably didn't hurt at all. As they hit at each other, both were screaming bloody murder*.

Lisa and her friends came skating over to where Murph and Butch were beating on each other, and Lisa started crying, "Stop hitting him! Leave Butch alone!"

Her friends were hugging her like she was the one in the fight.

Carl and Denise were skating down the river to the lake, holding hands, when Carl sped up and started yelling, "Whoop him, Butch!"

"SHUT UP, IDIOT!" a boy I had never seen before yelled from on top of the sandstone cliff. He looked to be about my brother's age.

"WHO YOU TELLING TO SHUT UP?" Carl scowled.

Denise pulled on Carl's coat, "Come on, don't get into it

*bloody murder - According to my dictionary, if you scream 'bloody murder,' you scream loudly due to pain or fright. 'Bloody' is described as: 1. covered, smeared, or running with blood. Murder is: the unlawful premeditated killing of one human being by another.

141

with that guy. Let's just have fun!"

"Who is *that* guy?" I asked Tony.

"That's Murph's big brother. He lives with their dad. He's just visiting. I don't think your brother wants to mess with him. I heard he was in juvie** for a while for fighting when they lived in Chicago."

"What do you mean, he lives with his dad? Doesn't his dad live with his mom?"

"No, they're divorced."

Weird, I thought. I'd never been to Murph's house, so I really didn't know too much about him. "But, didn't I see his dad that one time?"

"Yeah, that's his stepdad. Their mom lives here with him."

I looked back at my brother. Denise looked tense. My brother looked at her then looked back up at the boy who was challenging him.

"You shut up, loser. Who're you anyway?"

"The guy who's gonna kick your..."

Denise said, "Seriously Carl, if you are going to start something with that guy, I am leaving..."

"Start something? He started it..." Carl pleaded and followed Denise onto the lake, away from the guy up on the cliff.

What was with all the guys? They were all falling in love or something dumb like that. Then I thought of how cool it would be if Amy lived here in my neighborhood.

**juvie is short for 'Juvenile Hall, a place where they put a person below a specific age (18 in most countries) who has committed a crime.*

"CHICKEN!" Murph's brother hollered and threw a snowball at my brother, hitting Denise on the back.

"Now you've done it. You're gonna be sorry!" Carl yelled.

Denise shrugged it off. "I mean it, Carl. I don't like fighting or boys who do!"

"Then she must not like Butch or Murph..." I whispered and we started laughing, watching them rolling around on the ice, throwing punches and growling at each other.

"No one likes your stupid war games, oof!" Butch snarled.

Murph ducked a punch and threw one of his own.

"Whocareswhatyousay,you'rejustasissyanwhuu..." Murph hollered.

"SHUT UP!"

"Make me!"

Andy poked me in the ribs and made a farting sound with his mouth and arm and said, "Phhhhttt...you're made!"

I must have heard that one a million times, but it still always cracks me up. I looked down the canyon, and Carl and Murph's brother were closing in on each other. Denise was standing at the side of the frozen river where a group of girls were.

Meanwhile, Sawyer had hiked all the way up to the top of the hill and pushed himself off from the fence at the top. "I waxed these good, so I am going to fly SOOOOOOOO high!" he yelled as he started to come down the hill.

I turned to see Sawyer sailing down the hill.

Tony yelled, "SAWYER, YOU'RE GOING TOO FAST! YOU'RE GONNA..."

Everyone turned to watch him as Sawyer burned down the hill twice as fast as anyone had, then catapulted off the jump and flew straight up for about a mile through the air.

"HEY, HEY, WATCH THIS YOU GUYS, WOOOOOEEEEE..."

Murph and Butch stopped punching each other and just stood there with their mouths hanging open. My brother and Denise were watching too, and Murph's brother had finished climbing down the icy cliff and was heading right for my brother, who had his back to him.

Sawyer started falling fast and face first. One of the skis caught an edge when he came down and face planted him with his arms sticking straight out when he hit. His head snapped like a limp doll's, and he just lay there groaning and crying out, "I can't move my arms!" When he tried to stand up, both of his wrists were bent really weird and he fell back down.

Everyone started running up the hill to where Sawyer lay face down groaning and crying, "I..., it hurts so bad!"

I stayed behind to see what was going to happen to Carl, but I still could hear everyone's voices rumbling down onto the lake.

"Carl, watch out behind you!" I yelled just as Murph's big brother snuck up on my brother while he was distracted by Sawyer's fall. My brother spun around and hit Murph's brother right in the jaw with a closed fist. That was the day the legend began about Carl; the kid with one punch knocked out the kid who'd already been in juvie.

Denise spun around and said, "I'm so outta here! Carl, I told you I don't like fighting!"

"What was I supposed to do? He attacked me!" Carl pleaded. Murph's big brother was lying on the ice, groaning.

"Don't follow me!" Denise yelled. "Just stay here with all your stupid friends and see if you can all beat each other up."

Murph's big brother groaned loud and slowly sat up, rubbing his jaw. "Pretty good sucker punch, dude." He smiled, showing a missing tooth. It was obvious that this wasn't his first fight.

Carl looked at him with a puzzled look on his face. "Sucker punch? You were jumping me!"

Murph's brother extended his hand and said, "Help me up?"

"Yeah, right! Then what, on the way up you punch me in the face? You think I'm an idiot?"

"Heck no. Don't want another one of your roundhouses in the kisser," he laughed.

I thought, man, that is one tough guy. I've been punched by Carl and believe me it hurts!

Carl held his hand out, and Murph's brother grabbed it and hoisted himself up.

"Name's Boney. Boney Murphy."

"BONEY?"

"Yeah, I used to be really skinny." He smiled really wide. "So, folks just called me Boney, and it stuck."

"Carl Peters." My brother shook his hand.

"Good to meet you, mate. You got a great punch there. Ever consider taking up boxing?"

I couldn't believe my ears. My brother had just sent that Boney kid flying, and that seemed to make him like Carl instead of

hate him, like you would think.

"Nah... so, what's your real name?"

"I'll pass. Don't want to go into that. Just call me Boney. Now what's there to do around this place?"

I turned around again when Sawyer, who was still lying and moaning in the snow, started to cry, "I really can't move my hands! HELP!"

I ran up the hill and joined everyone else up there, who were gathered around Sawyer in a circle. Blood was leaking out of his nose, and his hands were turned around in a weird angle. Sawyer's face was pale white, and he looked like he was about to barf.

"We b-b-better get S-Sawyer's m-mom down h-h-here. I th-think he is r-really hurt!" Andy sputtered, looking right at me.

"Go, Peters, run!" Butch yelled.

And I did.

A little while later Sawyer's dad pulled his pickup truck in as close to the lake as he could get, and then carried Sawyer from the slope to his truck. Everyone kind of just left, going every which direction. I guess there had been enough action that it was time to call it a day.

I took the long way around the lake and heard some whispering. I recognized one of the voices, so I tiptoed to these rocks that looked down into the hidden canyon where the voices were coming from. As I peeked over the cliff edge, I couldn't believe my eyes. Butch was sitting down there holding hands with Lisa, and she was giggling at every thing he said. Man oh man, what was the Secret Brotherhood of Boys going to think about that?

The next day Sawyer showed up at my house with a swollen face and two casts, one on each arm. His left arm was in a sling.

"I broke both wrists and my collarbone." Sawyer said with a smile on his face that told me he was kind of proud of himself. "Dad says this is my ninth, tenth and eleventh broken bone."

"Does it hurt?" I asked.

"Heck, yeah, it hurts, but did you see the air I caught?"

We both laughed and went inside.

We were watching the television when the doorbell rang. I went to the door and it was Butch. "Hey, loverboy, how's it going?"

"Shut up, Peters, we need to talk."

"Okay, Sawyer's here."

"Then it can wait."

Butch moved past me, kicked his boots off at the front door and stole my chair in front of the television.

CHAPTER NINETEEN

The Footh Tairy

So, my front tooth came out last Friday. YEAH! Finally I lost a tooth that shows!

All the other kids in my class have lost a whole mouthful, but I have been waiting and waiting and have only lost a couple. Mom says I am a late bloomer* and that I am younger than everyone in my class by a whole year, but there were first graders losing teeth when I was in first grade and mine just weren't budging.

I wiggled my tooth back and forth so much in the last couple of days that I think it's all I did. I just couldn't stop until it finally started to wiggle loose.

I was scared that it was going to hurt really bad, because one of my friends told me his front teeth hurt really bad when he pulled them. But then again, he went on to say that his dad had pulled it out with a thick piece of yarn and it cut his gums. It made me shudder to think about it. Mine only stung for about five seconds, and that was it.

It is the weirdest thing. No matter how hard I try not to let it, my tongue keeps finding its way back to the hole where my tooth

*late bloomer (with adj.), a person who matures or flourishes at a specified time: he was a late bloomer.

was. For the first day it tasted like sucking on a metal pipe and the blood got down into my stomach and made me feel kind of sick and dizzy, but that is all past now.

My dad keeps calling me a 'toothless wonder', and I can tell he is proud of me. He says things like, "My Gabe, is growing up," and, "Pretty soon you will be a full-grown man, buddy." I like my dad a lot!

Now I kind of look like a jack-o-lantern from Halloween. Losing the tooth makes me talk kind of funny. The first time I talked about the Tooth Fairy coming, I said the 'Footh Tairy' and everyone cracked up.

The coolest thing is that I put that tooth under my pillow, and the next morning there was a crisp dollar bill and the tooth had vanished. Now, I don't know really know what to think about the Tooth Fairy and all, but I do know that dollar came out of nowhere and I had heard all about the Tooth Fairy, which kind of scared me to think that some weird stranger was going to fly into our house and steal my teeth.

Some people say parents put the money under your pillow, so to make sure it wasn't one of my parents who put it there, I had pushed my dresser in front of my door and the dresser was in the same place in the morning! So, there was no way my parents could have taken that tooth and left a dollar.

A dollar for a tooth is a lot of dough, as much as I can make in a week, so I got this genius idea. If I could make the same amount for a tooth that I made earning my allowance by doing chores, I should just pull out all of my teeth and then I can get the Hot Wheels track and the Legos bucket I really want, and maybe some of the Hot Rod trading cards, too. The other thing is that then all of my grown-up teeth would come in, and I wouldn't look like such a little kid in my class anymore.

When you are losing a tooth, everyone has advice about how to get it pulled. My grandpa called and told me his old trick, "Gabriel, my boy, you push in, not pull out. That breaks the flesh connection, and it doesn't tear out any so it doesn't hurt."

The flesh connection? Gross me out, Gramps.

My friends all had their opinions too, and each told me how they lost their teeth. My dad told me his stories which sounded really gruesome on account of the fact that he had ten older brothers and sisters, and the brothers, my uncles, figured out new ways every day to torment him and threaten his teeth, whether they were ready to come out or not. I figured I was lucky - I mean, after all, I just have Carl to beat up on me. One thing is for sure, everyone has teeth pulling stories.

Carl offered to bash me in the mouth with his fist to make it easy, which of course I turned down immediately and slammed my bedroom door right on his face and locked it, which made him really mad. He was pounding on it and yelling so loud that Mom came up the stairs and yelled at him.

A few minutes later I heard some bumping noises coming from the front of the house, which I recognized as the same noises that used to wake me up in the middle of summer, back when we shared the same bedroom and Carl would crawl up onto the roof to sneak back into our bedroom after being down the street messing around with his friends. When I caught him climbing up the roof to try to sneak into my bedroom window to get me back, I locked the window and pushed my rear end with only my tighty-whitey underwear on up against the window and started wiggling my butt around, mooning him and cracking myself up.

He started yelling that he was going to kill me if he could get his hands on me, which just made me laugh even harder. I was laughing so hard at my own joke that I fell right out of the upper bunk and onto the floor, knocking my elbow hard on the dresser, which made my funny bone go wild.

As I lay there moaning and wondering if I broke anything in the fall, my stuffed squirrel, Deeden, landed on top of my head, which gave me another idea. I pulled some vampire blood out of my top dresser drawer and dripped it onto Deeden's face. I could hear Carl climbing down off the roof, giving up for now anyway. I looked out my window to see him going down the street.

I opened my door and tiptoed over to Carl's room and set my now-bloody squirrel on top of Carl's pillow. For some reason my big, hairy, scary brother is afraid of my little defenseless stuffed squirrel, and I can't help myself. I figured Carl wouldn't be back in his room until it was time for bed, and by then his room would be pitch black. When he switched his desk lamp on it would shine on Deeden's face, which would make him look like a vampire squirrel.

I couldn't wait to hear the fireworks from that one.

I spent about an hour now wiggling every one of my teeth, trying to see if I could pull them out one by one to make a bunch of dough. I got tired of it after a while, and started building with my Legos and drawing some pictures in my Big Chief notebook. The doorbell rang and I could hear Andy coming up the stairs toward my room.

"What's the password?"

"You are a turd brain?"

"NOPE, you are!"

I flung the door open and jumped on Andy, pulling him to the floor where we wrestled around, knocking things all over the place.

"BOYS! WHAT ON EARTH ARE YOU DOING UP THERE MAKING ALL THAT RACKET?"

"Nothing, Mom, just goofing around... sorry."

I closed the door and put my finger to my lips. Andy and I spent the rest of the afternoon playing monopoly.

When bedtime came I was all settled in when I heard this blood-curdling scream coming from Carl's room. I started to laugh really hard into my pillow when I heard this weird scratching sound at my door and around the knob. Suddenly my door, which I had locked for this very reason, came springing open.

"YOU CHICKEN-DUNCE, I CAN PICK YOUR LOCK, AND NOW YOU'RE GOING DEAD!" Carl came in and jumped up onto the upper bunk, sending poor Flopster bawling and sprawling. Then Carl was smothering me with his big, ugly body.

I couldn't move, and then he started to give me a major Indian rug burn. It hurt so bad I thought my arm was going to twist off. Then he turned his attention to my head and started to give me noogies. When it felt like he had rubbed off almost all of my hair he pulled my pajama bottoms upward so hard he gave me an atomic wedgie supreme.

"That'll teach you to moon me, you chicken-butt!' he growled into my ear.

He was giving me everything he had all at once, and he was doing it all with one hand while holding his other hand over my mouth so I couldn't scream for Mom or Dad.

"You see what happens to pesky little chicken-dorks when they think they are so smart?" he was whispering into my ear when suddenly he gave me a wet-willy, which is always the worst from him because he loads his finger up with so much spit that you can't get it out of your ear, ever, which totally grosses me out.

I bit down on Carl's hand hard, and he jumped back, sending him falling off the upper bunk onto the ground and screaming, "You chicken-sissy, boys don't bite!"

This wasn't true, since I'm a boy and I had just chomped down on his hand pretty good. Carl was making so much noise that within a few seconds Dad was bounding up the stairs to see what was going on.

"What in tarnation is going on up here?" Dad stood in the doorway with a mean look on his face.

That one always cracks me up. What is 'tarnation' anyway?

I tried to look as wounded as I could and hung my head off the upper bunk, moaning as if Carl had just pounded me.

"Nothing, Dad, we were just playing around, right, Gabe?"

Carl gave me one of his warning looks, like if I didn't go along with it, what he was just doing to me would be a party compared to what would come next.

"Uh, I uh..."

I couldn't think straight, my head was ringing, my pajamas were still wedged deeply where the sun doesn't shine and my ear was full of stupid-Carl drool. If that was playing around, what was fighting?

"I uh..."

"We were playing, right, Gabe?"

Carl flashed me another one of his looks that could kill.

"Well, stop your playing around. It is time to go to bed. It is past time. Carl, go back to your own room and go to sleep," said Dad.

"But he..."

"No buts, Carl! GO NOW!"

"GOSH, how come little chicken-golden boy doesn't ever get in trouble, and I always do?"

"Well, Carl, no one said anyone was in trouble, and you are in Gabe's room, aren't you?"

Dad headed back down the stairs, and I could see that Carl had been standing still on the opposite side of his room from his bed, where Deeden was still propped up on his pillow, bleeding all over it by now.

When Dad was safely downstairs, Carl pulled a blanket off his bed without going near the pillows or Deeden and crept over to the bathroom. I knew it was going to be a long, uncomfortable night in the bathtub for poor Carl. I also know that somehow he would get me back for it.

I tried to pull my teeth out with a string and with the door. It budged just a little bit but I need to pull much more!

SLAM

ouch!

I slipped out of my room and got Deeden back. I wiped the vampire blood off of his face and returned him to his place on my dresser, then thought twice and grabbed him and cuddled with him and Flopster until all three of us were sound asleep in my comfy bed.

CHAPTER TWENTY

The Tooth Thief

The next day I got back to the business of making money from my teeth. I got a piece of string out of Mom's drawer and tied it to my doorknob and around one of my teeth. It wouldn't budge. I tried all of the teeth in my mouth and none of them were coming out, but man oh man did that make my eyes water.

"OWWW..." I moaned, lying on my back. It stung every time I pushed that string down between my teeth, and then even worse when I slammed the door. This was a silly idea, but I really needed that money. Again I had that metallic taste from the blood that oozed out between my teeth from all the yanking and pulling.

Carl was across the hall in his room and still burning mad at me for last night. I guess when I kept slamming the door to try to pull my teeth out it got annoying because he came over to my room to investigate.

"What the heck are you doing, chicken-butthead? By the way, I am so going to get you good for last night."

"Ohhh, you said the -h-word. I am telling!"

"Shut up, chicken-stupid," he snarled.

Wow, Carl was going for broke - 'stupid,' 'shut up' AND the

H-word. Mom would get him good if she heard that.

"You're in a great mood today, *nice* big brother," I taunted him.

"You'd be in a bad mood if you had a chicken-dunce-dork-head little brother to bug you all the time, too."

"Shut your door if you don't like it."

"You shut your mouth, chicken-pipsqueak. What are you trying to pull, anyway? What's with all the noise?"

"Carl, stop talking like that," Mom called up the stairs.

"See what you did, you got me in trouble, you chicken-squirt," Carl tried to whisper in a low growl.

"Carl, I can hear you," Mom called up again.

"Sheesh, how come butthead chicken-dunce can go around slamming doors and making all kinds of racket and no one ever says anything to him? How come I am always the one getting in trouble?"

"Carl, don't talk back to me!" Mom yelled up.

"Jeez, why don't you just tell me he is your favorite?"

Carl slammed his door louder than any of my tooth-pulling noise. I could hear Mom coming up the stairs; this was going to be good. He'd said some of Mom's totally worst favorite words out loud, and to her!

"Carl!" Mom whispered at his door. "Carl, may I come in?"

"It's a free country, isn't it?" Carl snarled.

Mom opened his door, entered, and closed the door behind her.

I jumped down off my bunk bed, where I had climbed to be away from the fireworks, but now with the door closed I couldn't hear what was going on in there. I pushed my ear up onto his door and listened.

"Carl, you know I don't like it when you talk to your little brother like that, or anyone for that matter."

"But, he is always so annoying, Mom," Carl whined.

"I understand how annoying a brother can be, believe me. I was the only girl! You know how bad Uncle Stewie and Uncle Howie can be?"

"Yeah, that wouldn't be fun when you were a kid. They act like idiots now!" Carl laughed.

Mom laughed too. "Imagine Dad growing up with Uncle Morris."

Carl started to laugh harder at the thought. "Yeah, he must have taught Dad every bad word in the book when they were kids."

"That's an understatement. I swear, that man..." Mom's voice trailed off and suddenly the room was totally quiet, like somehow they knew I was on the other side of the door listening to their private conversation. I backed away, and they started to talk in lower voices.

"You don't have to swear, Mom, Uncle Morris takes care of that."

They both started laughing at how ridiculous my uncle's language was, and at Carl's quick wit.

They went on and on like that for a while and I started to really feel left out. I tried to think of what I could do that would make enough noise to make them curious so they would come talk to me.

I went back to my room and shut the door. I had to stick to my plan and figure out how I was going to make some extra spending money. After a little while Mom came out of Carl's room, and then I heard snoring coming from Carl's room. I peeked in his door and saw him sprawled out on his bed sleeping, with Flop curled up next to him. Suddenly an idea hit me, and I raced across the hall to my room. I would try the evil squirrel trick again - he wouldn't expect me to do it so soon again.

I tiptoed back into Carl's room and positioned Deeden, who had just a bit of newly-applied vampire blood on his lips right by Flop, and turned his lamp on so it highlighted him. When my brother woke up, my Vampire Squirrel would be staring at him.

I bounded downstairs, "Mom, how come Carl sleeps so much?"

"He's going through a growth spurt. That's part of the reason he is so grouchy all the time."

"And the other part is that he is just a jerk?"

"Gabe, that's not nice."

"*He's* not nice."

I grabbed a snack and went back up to my room to plan.

I started to give up on the idea of making my fortune with pulled teeth, when a strange coincidence happened.

I went down to Tony's house. Tony has gobs and gobs of people in his family. Tony and I were down in the basement practicing for our new band when his mom called down the stairs, "Gabriel, would you like to stay for dinner?"

I looked at Tony as if to ask if he wanted me to. He just shrugged and nodded.

"I would love to, thank you, Mrs. Carlson!"

She walked down the basement stairs. "We are having corn on the cob, and I know that can be tough for someone who doesn't have a front tooth. Do you want me to cut the corn off? Lord knows eating it could pull the rest of your teeth!"

I spun around. "Really?"

"Really what, Gabriel?" She looked at me like I had three heads.

"Could corn on the cob really pull my teeth out?" I didn't even realize it, but I was dancing around at the thought of it.

Tony and his mom looked at me like I had three heads.

"I need to lose some more teeth and fast! Could I have two ears of corn, please?"

"Well, that's fine, Gabriel, but why do you want to lose your teeth so fast?"

"It's kind of a long story," I muttered under my breath, hoping to change the subject.

Tony's mom nodded, then she started up the stairs back to the kitchen. She called down the stairs again, "Gabriel, you need to call your mother to make sure it is okay with her that you stay for dinner."

"Okay!" I yelled back up to her.

I called Mom on this old-fashioned phone. It was supposed to be the kind they used in England to go with Tony's dad's special bar that was supposed to be from a place called Pub.

After Mom said it would be fine as long as I used all of my "yes, please" and "thank you" manners, I went upstairs to the kitchen to tell Tony's mom. Tony stayed in his room, working words for a song we were planning to play for his mom and dad after dinner.

Tony's mom was standing at the kitchen sink, humming some old-fashioned, corny love song. "My mom said it was okay for me to stay, and thank you again for asking me." Tony's mom was always really nice. She nodded, but just kept humming.

Now, here is where the coincidence came in. I noticed these weird little metal boxes that she kept up on the windowsill right in front of her. "What are those for?"

She smiled and told me that there was one for each kid in Tony's family, and they are filled with lost teeth. What a rip-off, I thought. Tony's mom had been keeping all of those teeth so the poor kids probably never put them under their pillows.

Losing teeth is kind of like having a pop can. You get to use the pop inside, and then you can turn the can in for money. You get to use the teeth, and then they are worth something when they come out. All those teeth on the windowsill were unredeemed! There must have been a thousand teeth in all of those boxes, and they were each still worth a dollar apiece!

I got an idea. "Why do you have all of these teeth? Aren't you supposed to put them under the pillow for the tooth fairy*?"

"Um... Uhh... Actually, Gabriel, these teeth were under the kid's pillows. I made a deal with the tooth fairy to get them back. I know it is kind of weird, but I wanted them for my little boxes. So the kids got fifty cents apiece, and I got the teeth."

"Weird."

"What?"

"That's kind of weird to collect people's teeth, don't you think?"

Now some people might think it is kind of shady to talk to a kid's mom like that, but Tony's mom had always been real upfront and easy to talk to, so it was comfortable to ask her questions and to call her weird. She just smiled when I said it, and didn't get mad like some of the other guy's moms would or Mean Mrs. Rickles. I can't even imagine ever talking to her, let alone calling her 'weird' to her face and surviving.

Thinking about her made me sad for her and Ryan. I didn't really like them at all, but they were really going through a tough time.

Anyways, I got this idea. I knew it wasn't too nice, but after all, they were just old teeth. How valuable could they really be to someone who wasn't putting them under a pillow?

Tony's family has this covered back porch area on their house. It is connected to the kitchen by a door, but it is enclosed in the winter and cold months (it opens up to be like a regular patio in the summer and warm months). That was where we helped Tony's mom set the table.

---

*Tooth Fairy -noun: a fairy said to leave a gift, esp. a coin, under a child's pillow in exchange for a baby tooth that has fallen out and been put under the pillow.

She was out there the whole time directing us. Every time I went back into the kitchen, I opened one of those little metal boxes and pulled a couple teeth out. By the time I worked my way down the little line of boxes I had about a dozen teeth clattering around in my front pocket. It was kind of gross to think that the teeth in my pocket at one time had been connected inside all those mouths, but I had a really good plan for them.

That night I put one of the teeth under my pillow, and when I went downstairs to say goodnight I whispered in my mom's ear that I had finally lost another tooth. She looked happy about it, and all I could think of was how this would be easy money.

The next morning I awakened to find another dollar under my pillow and the tooth gone. As my eyes adjusted to being opened, I scanned my room and saw that somehow someone with a bent coat hook had hung my stuffed squirrel from my overhead light. Whoever it was also had used Mom's lipstick to draw huge lips on him, and put blue eye gunk around his eyes, and pierce a pair of mom's dangling earrings through Deeden's ear and his nose.

I guess my Vampire Squirrel doesn't scare my big brother the way he used to. I would have to come up with something else.

I waited for a few days, and then announced at the dinner table that I had another tooth to go under the pillow. Dad said something about me catching up with the other kids in my grade, and I felt kind of bad. I was lying about my teeth, and my parents were happy for me.

A few days later I told my mom that another tooth would be heading under my pillow that night.

Mom looked at me with kind of a concerned face. "Gabriel, you aren't pulling these teeth out too early are you?"

"Mom, don't worry, everything is just fine."

"It really is important to let your teeth come out when they are ready. Let me look at your mouth, Gabe."

"Uh, Mom, I just remembered, I haven't cleaned up the dog messes in the yard. I will be right back." I bounded out into the backyard, leaving Mom standing there with her mouth open and a very curious look on her face.

While I was wandering around the yard, feeling guilty about lying to my mom and making money from it, a brainstorm hit. I knew what I could do to get Carl really good. I would take the stinkbug jar and hide it behind a book on his bookshelf. He never went near books that he didn't have to read, so it would sit there stinking the place up for a long time. I was also going to take the chicken head from Gran's farm that had been wrapped in a paper towel waiting for an idea to hit, and put it under Carl's pillow.

Mom watched me from the kitchen window. I saw that she had the phone cradled under her chin and panicked. I ran back into the house.

"Mom, who are you talking to?"

"Gabe, shhh, I am on the phone." Mom motioned furiously in the air with her hand at me. "I just thought that since you had Gabe over for dinner the other night, that I would ask if Tony could join us. I am making sloppy joe's and I know those are his favorite."

Sweat trickled down my back. This was my worst nightmare. Mom was talking to Tony's mom. What if the subject of my teeth came up? What if she'd noticed the teeth were gone? What if...

Mom hung up the phone and walked over to where I was standing. "I thought you were cleaning the backyard. Why are you acting so strangely?"

"It's nothing, Mom, I just wanted to, uh, I was thinking..."

"Okay, young man, something's up. I can tell. Follow me." Mom led me into the living room and sat on the couch. I followed her with that sinking feeling in my stomach.

"Spill it..." she commanded.

Now, one thing I know about Mom - because I have watched it more than once with Carl - is that if she gives you a chance to come clean and you do, it usually goes easier on you, but if she gives you a chance to come clean and you don't, she will get madder at the fact that you are lying even more than the thing you are lying about. "Well, I uh... You see... When I..."

"Gabe, just tell me what is going on."

Her face was so serious I was feeling very ashamed of myself.

"Well, you know when I lost my first tooth and got a dollar?"

"Mmm hmmm."

Mom waited patiently for me to continue.

"I, uh, well, when the tooth fairy brought me a dollar for that tooth, I mean a whole dollar, which is my whole allowance for a week, I couldn't believe it, so I started to try to pull my teeth. Then, when none would come out, I tried Frisky, but he didn't want me to pull his teeth and so, I found some teeth and..."

"You found some teeth? What on earth does that mean? Where does one go to find teeth?"

Mom always talked like an professor when she was serious.

"I don't want to say."

"Young man, I think you better. Do you mean to tell me that the last several teeth that you claimed to have lost weren't yours?"

"Right," I muttered to the floor.

"Gabriel, what on earth has gotten in to you. That is stealing."

"Which part?"

"What do you mean, 'which part?' Which part could I be talking about?"

"Uh, the part about where I got the teeth, or the part about me getting a dollar for the teeth that weren't mine. BUT, can't the Tooth Fairy afford it? I mean, there must be millions of teeth lost every day around the world. What's a few more?"

"Gabriel Robin Peters, what on earth are you talking about? You cannot justify stealing on the grounds that since there are so many others, your crimes don't count."

"Crimes? You think I am a criminal now, Mom?"

My bottom lip started to quiver, and tears filled my eyes. The last thing I ever wanted is for my mom to not be proud of me.

"I'm sorry, Mom, I just wanted that Hot Wheels track so bad, I wasn't thinking..."

"What Hot Wheels track are you talking about now? What does that have to do with the price of tea in China?"

"What?" I had no idea what Mom was talking about tea and China for.

"Never mind, it is just a saying. Go on, you were going to tell me about where you got the teeth."

Mom folded her arms and sat back in the sofa looking even more serious now, so I knew I was trapped. I was going to have to come clean, and any more delay was just going to make it worse.

I spilled the whole story, about how I had taken teeth from the boxes on Tony's mom's windowsill.

At times Mom looked like she was going to laugh, and at times she looked so mad I was glad she wasn't the hitting kind of mom. When I finished I just sat there staring at my feet.

"Go get the teeth."

Mom stood over me now.

"Why?"

"Gabriel, go get all of the teeth that you stole from Mrs. Carlson."

Hearing Mom say the word 'stole' just killed me. I had never been more ashamed of myself. A thief is something that I never wanted to be. What was the big deal? They were just lousy old teeth. It isn't like I took something of any value to anyone.

But somehow I knew I was trying to convince myself of that. Moms seem to value everything about their kids, unless their kid is a thief like me.

I went up to my room and got the teeth from where I had hidden them under my Snoopy piggy bank.

Carl came into my room.

"Oh man, I was standing up here in the hall listening to that whole thing. Man, you have had it. Dad is going to kill you, chicken-thief!"

I pushed past Carl without saying a word. I was so ashamed of myself I just had no fight left in me. That was twice I was called a 'thief,' and I never knew how bad that could feel.

I walked downstairs where Mom was waiting, and held my hand out, my eyes welling up.

"Oh no, not to me, young man. You need to give those back

to Mrs. Carlson."

Mom also handed me the teeth that I had claimed were mine.

"But, how did you get these mom? I left them for the..."

"I, uh, I was, uh, I was..."

"Never mind." I muttered, already kind of having doubts about the whole thing anyway. I didn't need more bad news.

Mom walked to the front door and opened it. Then she walked me down to Tony's house and waited on the curb.

I walked up to the front door and knocked. When Mrs. Carlson came to the door, I thought I was going to die. My lips were quivering and my hands were shaking.

"I'm sorry, Mrs. Carlson, these are yours."

"What on earth?"

"I am a thief. I am so sorry. I'll understand if you never want to see me again."

Mrs. Carlson looked from me to my mom, and then back at me with a strange look on her face. "You took these from my boxes Gabriel?"

"Yes."

Tears started to well up in my eyes again, and then splashed down over my cheeks.

"But why?" Mrs. Carlson looked hurt.

Tony came bounding up behind her, "Hey Gabe, uh, wow, what's wrong? Someone die?"

"Tony, hush." Mrs. Carlson stood, waiting for my explanation.

I just stood there. I couldn't say another word.

Mrs. Carlson finally barked at Tony, "Young man, go back to the kitchen. I am talking to Gabriel right now!"

"Sheesh, you don't have to yell at me, Mom, I didn't do anything!"

Tony stomped off in a huff.

Now I had really done it. I was a thief, I had made one of my best buddies mad and Mom was ashamed of me. I just wanted this day to end, and fast!

Mom came walking up to the front door and listened to me as I explained myself to Mrs. Carlson. There were a few times that their eyes met and they both looked like they found something really funny, but as far as I was concerned there was nothing funny about this, and one thing I knew for sure: I would never, ever, ever steal another thing for the rest of my life no matter how bad I wanted a Hot Wheels track or anything else.

Mrs. Carlson listened to my explanation and my apology and then suddenly she bent down and hugged me tight. "Don't worry about it dear. What's done is done and you've said you are sorry and that's that. We won't speak of this again." Mom and Mrs. Carlson looked at each other and smiled.

Later, I put the money back on Mom's dresser, even the dollar I got for my actual tooth. I wondered how she would get it back to the Tooth Fairy and hoped I never had to speak of the whole stupid thing again, just like Mrs. Carlson had said.

Here is the weirdest thing about the whole tooth-stealing incident. Mom never told Dad. Carl never said another word about it, and Tony wasn't even mad at me.

But it would be a while before I would go back to Tony's house because of how ashamed I felt, even though Mrs. Carlson told me she forgave me.

Several days later when the whole thing had blown over I went through with my plan to plant the stinkbugs and chicken head in Carl's room. I sneaked in there and did the deed. When I opened the jar of stinkbugs, I thought I was going to puke all over Carl's room it smelled so bad. The smell spread quickly, and I figured by the time Carl came home it would be so bad he wouldn't be able to stand it in there and would have to sleep in the bathtub.

I decided I would blame it on his smelly socks if anyone asked me what it was. Then I headed outside so I wouldn't be around when Carl came home to find the disgusting smell or nasty chicken head.

Several hours later, I came in from playing outside and could smell the stinkbugs upstairs from the bottom of the stairs. It was disgusting, and I didn't know if I was going to be able to stand smelling them as I got closer to his room. I ducked into my room and started laughing at what a mean prank it was. If it smelled this strong in the hall and my own room, how bad it must be in his.

I couldn't stand the stench anymore, and when I went out into the hall Flop was lying on the carpet chewing on something.

"What are you doing Flopster?"

It didn't look like one of his mice that he was chewing on, so I tugged on it. He gave out a low growl as I pulled it away from him, and then I noticed he was chewing on the dried-up chicken head and it had a string tied to it. I looked up and saw that the frayed end of string hanging from my overhead light was the same as the string around the chicken head. But I hadn't tied a string to it...?

Then I realized Flop had pulled it down, and that it had been hanging right in front of my door. I slowly opened Carl's door, and realized there was no strong smell of stinkbugs in his room. Then I put my head back in my own room, and it was disgusting. I followed the smell and it got stronger by the bunk beds. I sniffed along the mattress and when I got to my pillow I thought I would throw up. I lifted my pillow and found the nasty black beetles spread out right there on my sheets and a note that said,

THOUGHT YOU MIGHT WANT THESE BACK,

CHICKEN-BACKFIRE!

HA HA, LOVE AND KISSES,

YOUR SMARTER BROTHER, CARL.'

What a terrible week it had been.

CHAPTER TWENTY-ONE

Valentine's Day

I was sitting on the floor of my bedroom decorating my shoebox for all of the Valentines I was hoping to get in class when Carl popped his big, ugly head around the door.

"Hey chicken-punk, Mom wants to see you right now. Man, you are in so much trouble!"

It felt like a big, hairy caterpillar had crawled up my back. "What happened? What'd I do?"

Carl just ignored me. Shrugging, he walked across the hall and closed his bedroom door.

My stomach started to flip-flop. I just hated being in trouble, especially with Mom. What had I done now?

I walked into the kitchen timidly where Mom was standing. "Hi, Mom, what's up?"

"Hi, Gabe. I'm just making dinner. What's up with you?"

Mom was smiling, and didn't look like she was mad at me at all.

"Uh, nothing. Carl said you wanted to see me?"

172

"No, I didn't say anything of the kind. Why would he say that?"

"I dunno. He said I was in major trouble."

"Well, should you be?"

"NO!"

"I'm just kidding, I haven't even seen your brother for the past hour or so. What is he up to now?"

I just shrugged, relieved that I wasn't in trouble. Just then Carl passed by the kitchen door and made a hand movement indicating that I had just been fooled. "HA HA, CHICKEN-BOY!" he mouthed.

I mouthed, "BIG DEAL, STUPID!"

It seemed like he was going to try to prank me now every chance he got. Well, two could play at that game.

Carl's eyes got widely exaggerated, like he couldn't believe I'd use the S-word. He held his arms up, banging his fists together, punching one fist into his other cupped hand like he was warming up to punch me.

I rolled my eyes at him. "Do you need some help, Mom?"

Carl mouthed, "Do you need some help, Mom?" sarcastically. Then he mouthed, "Suck up!"

I mouthed, "SHUT UP, UGLY!"

"Sure, that's sweet, honey. Would you peel those carrots for me?"

Mom smiled and patted my head.

Mom stuck her head in the refrigerator, and Carl snarled in

a low enough voice that only I heard - or so he thought, "Oh honey, baby sweetie, what a CHICKEN-WUSS!"

"Carl, how many times do I have to tell you to STOP calling your little brother those names?

"Uh, sorry."

"No you are not sorry or you would stop doing it!" Mom barked.

"I was just kidding around."

"Gabe, would you also peel and cut this cucumber up for me?"

"Uh huh."

I stood at the counter next to Mom, peeling the carrots into the sink and flashing Carl dirty looks as he sat at the kitchen table pretending to be busy with the newspaper. "What about him? He could do something around here."

"Oh, he will. He is going to do all of the dishes," Mom said in a sweet voice.

"YOU DIE, CHICKEN-PUNK!" Carl snarled, angry with me for focusing attention on the fact that he wasn't helping with dinner.

"CARL, STOP CALLING GABE NAMES ALL THE TIME!"

"Oh, come on Mom, he can handle it. Something has to make him a man!"

"I mean it, Carl. You need to learn to be nice."

Flop jumped up into Carl's lap and he started to stroke his fur. "Hey big boy, you are so cute, who loves you Flopster..."

Carl looked at me, and I started to laugh at him.

"Oh, yeah, that's manly," I said smartly.

Mom said, "I think it is sweet the way Carl loves animals."

Carl stood up, brushing Flop off his lap, and stood looking out the back glass door.

"Hey, Mom?" I asked.

"Yes?"

I lowered my voice, hoping Carl wasn't paying any attention to us anymore. "Do you think I'll get any Valentines this year?"

"Who would give a chicken-dork like you a Valentine?" Carl sneered, poking his big, ugly face back into the kitchen.

"Carl, don't you have homework to do?" Mom stared him down. "Must you always torment your little brother?"

"YES, I MUST!" Carl yelled over his shoulder, laughing as he bounded up the stairs to his bedroom.

Last year, even though there was a rule that if you brought a Valentine for anybody, you brought a Valentine for everybody. I only got a few. Even those were kind of lame.

I did get one Valentine that was a joke card with a mean drawing of me with an eye patch that said, 'WILL YOU BE MY UGLYTINE?'

"Sure, all the kids think you are a great guy, right?"

"Well, I don't know about all of the kids, but I do actually have some friends at school now."

"Is there someone special you are thinking of?" Mom winked.

"Mo-om, come on..."

"Well, those little girls you ride to school with are awfully cute, with all that beautiful blond hair."

"YUCK! Are you kidding, Mom? They are GROSS-ME-OUTS!"

"Oh Gabe, that isn't nice. They are nice girls. They are always so polite when I drive them."

"Yeah, well, they aren't nice when their mom drives. Anyway, no, Mom, I don't like girls - you know that!"

"No girls?"

"Well, actually Mom..." I lowered my voice, "promise not to tell?"

"Promise." Mom crossed her heart.

"There's this one girl named Amy..."

Carl popped around the door, "Ewww... Gabey's got a girl-friend!"

He must have snuck down the stairs and was crouching down where we couldn't see him.

"MO-OM!" I looked at Mom, horrified.

"Carl, stop spying on people."

"It's a free country..."

"Don't sass me, young man! Stop being so annoying. Go to your room. Gabe is telling me something in confidence, and if I hear you teasing him about Amy you will be grounded!"

Just Mom saying her name out loud made me wince.

"Jeez, can't anybody take a joke around here? I'll be down at Greg's!" Carl barked.

"No, I said go to your room. You have homework to finish, young man, and..."

"But, Mom..."

"I'll make you a deal. You can go to Greg's if you finish your math and promise not to tell anyone anything about Gabe's secret, which you aren't supposed to know about anyway. And that means you can't tease him about her either. I mean it about you being grounded for that!"

"Who cares about Gabe's stupid girlfriend anyway?"

"She's not my girlfriend..." I spoke up.

"Duh, you're too ugly to have a girlfriend."

"Carl, what did I tell you about being mean to Gabe?"

"I don't care what he thinks, Mom." I then gave Carl the meanest look I could and taunted, "Tell Mom about your girlfriend, Denise-epoo."

"Forget it! You are such a jerk! Just drop it." Carl's face got all red.

"Denise? You mean that cute little girl down the street with the shag haircut*?" Mom said, looking amused.

"You need to learn when to just shut up, chicken-puke!"

"CARL, HOW MANY TIMES DO I HAVE TO TELL YOU..."

*shag haircut (noun), a thick, tangled hairstyle or mass of hair: her hair was cut short in a boyish shag | (as adj.), a shag cut. Popular in the 1970s.

"BYE!"

Carl bounded back up the stairs to his bedroom.

"So, let's get back to Amy." Mom smiled.

I told Mom about her. About how her golden hair flowed in the breeze, and how her ocean blue eyes were the prettiest (besides Mom's, of course) that I had ever seen. Mom suggested we make some heart-shaped sugar cookies with messages like you see on those candies, and I could give Amy a dozen to show her that she was more special than the other Valentines in my class.

I agreed to bake the cookies with Mom, just as long as my friends didn't find out about it.

Mom made me take some of the cookies to Mrs. Abernathy and her daughters. I told them they were all for Mrs. Abernathy so the girls wouldn't think I liked them.

When I carried the Valentines into my class, there was a small box sitting on my desk and several other envelopes.

On the back of the box it said:

TO: Gabe

FROM: Amy

WILL YOU BE MY VALENTINE?

I opened the box and it was filled with yummy chocolates. As I looked around I noticed that no one else had a box like this from Amy. I thought I was going to faint.

CHAPTER TWENTY-TWO

Farmers And The Deal

Mom said we looked like walking packs of dominoes when the boys lined up across from the girls in our uniforms of black slacks, black leather belts and shoes, and pressed white, long-sleeved button-down shirts and black ties. The girls were all in plaid green dresses and shiny black shoes with white socks. A bunch of moms were snapping shots as fast as the official photographer, and the whole place was buzzing around us like we were all movie stars or something.

The end of the year was coming and we were taking class pictures, so everyone had to look just perfect (which would be impossible if Sister Mary Claire was in the picture). Amy whispered in my ear that she wanted to stand next to me in the pictures, which made my stomach do a little flip-flop. That was when I realized I wouldn't be seeing Amy anymore either, when I went to the new school, and that made me kind of sad. Even though with just a few exceptions every time Amy and I saw each other after the Valentine's Day, we just kind of avoided talking or pretty much anything. Carl says that is how it is with younger kids; just when they decide they are boyfriend and girlfriend they stop talking to each other and get really awkward. If you ask me, watching Carl and Denise talk and look at each other is the most awkward thing in the world!

Mom and Dad had told me last weekend that next year I really will go to the Pioneer Ridge Elementary where Andy and my other friends go to, and that I would be a fifth grader AT LAST! They promised this time, and there was no way I was ever going to come back to this school!

Mom and the other moms finished taking pictures, which seemed to take forever, and then we all had some cake and ice cream outside in the courtyard. Then all of the moms left and we went back to having a lesson outside about science stuff, which I already knew more about than Sister Mary Claire did on the subject of bugs and habitat, so I just doodled and daydreamed until she was finally done boring everyone.

I didn't really feel too bad about leaving my friends at St. Joe's, because they weren't as good friends of mine as my buddies who went to the Pioneer Ridge Elementary School, and the very best part was NO MORE CAR POOL!!! NO MORE POODLE-PUFF HAIR MEANIES! I was finally going to get to ride the big, yellow bus.

So, that night after dinner I was in my bedroom and Carl came in and just flopped down in his old bed and started petting Flop. Then, in one of Carl's rare nice moments when he wasn't calling me chicken names, I told him about Amy and how she made my stomach feel all funny and my hands got kind of sweaty the few times she ever talked to me. He told me that he thought that it was cool that I was seeing that girls were cool, and that Denise made him feel the same way.

'Cool' was Carl's new word.

"I guess we're just growing up, little brother."

He punched me on the arm, friendly-like, and didn't even call me chicken-lover-boy or something totally gross like that, which I would have thought he would.

I punched him back on his arm and said, "Cool!" Then we played with my Legos, which we hadn't done together for a long, long time.

After pictures we were told that we could all go out to the playground and play for half an hour. That was when I sneaked across the street - under the street actually, through a tunnel. Across the street was Steelers Market. We were forbidden to go there during school hours, but I was on a special mission.

I crept into the candy aisle, always awatching for the nun's batwings hovering over their heads or for the swish of the priest's cloaks looking for boys who were off school grounds illegally.

I knew what I was doing was wrong, but it was a dare and I had taken the dare, so now I had no choice but to go. I grabbed handfuls of small boxes of candy, then pulled my shirt out and made a basket for the candy out of it. I ran to the clerk up at the checkout stand closest to the door and pulled out several severely-wrinkled dollar bills.

After he rang it all up, I stuffed the Atomic Fireballs, cinnamon Jolly Rancher sticks and other hot candies into my lunch bag.

The clerk looked at me sternly and nodded with his head, "You go to that school across the street, kid?"

I felt panicked. Would he call Mother Superior's office, or even worse, Monsignor* Cavanaugh's?

"Uh, yeah, but I...

"Relax, kid. I used to go there, too. Boys have always snuck through the tunnel to this store... for decades. I even did once, but got caught. I don't recommend that at all! That was back when a whupping was normal, everyday stuff, and they used rulers on us back in the day. See this here scar on the top of my hand..."

*Monsignor - the title of various senior Roman Catholic positions.

181

I nodded, watching the door and wanting to get out of there fast. "Look, I gotta be getting back. Maybe I can look at your scar another time, but... well... See ya!"

"Hey kid, you forgot your change! Kid!"

I turned for just a moment to see the clerk start heading toward me, but I sprinted as fast as I could past this funny old guy who was pushing a whole line of grocery carts. Then I just kept running through the parking lot toward the tunnel that would take me back below the street.

If I made it back through the tunnel without getting caught, I could huddle next to the huge church and hide in the ivy if someone came up the sidewalk. Then I had a plan to duck behind cars in the parking lot and get back onto campus without anyone knowing I was gone.

If I were caught going back through the campus, I would merely say I was in the church saying a few extra prayers that I would be a good boy that day, which would be a lie that I would have to talk about in confession**, which would cause a problem because I might be confessing to the very priest I had lied to.

I imagined a stern priest patting my head and suggesting that I, even though only a fourth grader, become the lead altar boy, a position of great importance in our school and our church. I would feel so ashamed of myself for getting rewarded when I knew I was doing something wrong on top of my lies.

I opened a small cardboard box and crunched down on the pee-wee, marble-sized Atomic Fireballs, savoring the heat on my tongue. The red candies turned my teeth, tongue and lips bright neon-red. We weren't supposed to eat candy at school, but technically I wasn't at school, but all of a sudden I felt panicked that the

**confession - In the Catholic church confession is made to a priest in a confessional, which is like a box with a screen so you and the priest can't see each other's face.

182

red color from the Atomic Fireballs would give me away.

I rounded the corner and could see that everyone had gone back inside, so I snuck down the ivy-covered walkway next to the big building, and as I slipped unnoticed back into the lunchroom, I devised a lie of having used the restroom if the awful Sister Mary Claire stopped me.

But that didn't happen, and all of the boys in the cafeteria looked at me with a certain admiration. I'd been brave enough to defy the stern rules, cross the street and retrieve what they all wanted. I had done the one dare no one else was willing to take. I had gone from the biggest fourth-grade zero last year to the biggest fourth-grade hero this year! I had just done a dare that even the toughest sixth grade boys had turned down.

Each of them sat with hand in pocket. Hard-earned allowances soon would be mine.

I started an auction, the boys bidding it up, competing for the candy that now sat in my lunch bag. I pulled out a box of Atomic Fireballs and shook it.

"Bidding starts at twenty-five cents, boys!"

The boys looked at the coveted holy grail of candy I had just paid a mere fifteen cents for.

When I stuck my tongue out to show the fire red color, Johnny Germain, a kid who was already getting acne in fourth grade, whisper-yelled with a squeaky, changing voice, "Twenty-five!"

Another boy, "Thirty!"

"Thirty-five!"

Johnny Germain punched the other bidder, "Forty! Come on, Jimmy, it's almost all I got! I just got to have me some of that hot stuff!"

"Don't worry, Johnny, I got lots more where that one came from!" I smiled, motioning down to the huge bulk hiding in my shirt.

"Yeah, but they're all gonna go higher that what I have." Johnny's voice creaked like a squeaky door.

"You could borrow!" someone said, and the bidding kept going.

Jimmy gave Johnny a too-bad-so-sad look, and yelled "Fifty!"

It was a bold move. Usually these moved quickly, but at nickel increments.

Johnny groaned, "Man, all I have is fifty. You stink, Jimmy!"

Out of the woodwork came Franky Farmers with a bid.

Farmers growled, "Fifty-five, and if you bid it higher, Jimmy, I will pulverize you when we go out on the playground!"

Farmers was the biggest fourth-grader ever in the history of St. Joe's, and he was a pretty nice guy - that is, if he liked you and I was lucky because he liked me.

A funny thing I found out about Farmers accidentally, that

I would never tell another soul, was when I went into the office one day. Mrs. Ward had a stack of manila folders sitting on her desk, and his was on top. Each folder had a tab with the student's full name and their school picture stapled to it. I couldn't believe Farmers's full name was Francis Ferdinand Farmers III. That had to be the most ridiculous name I had ever heard of, and he was the third one to have it! But like I said, I would never tell a living soul because I liked Farmers being on my side!

Farmers' face always looked sunburned, and it was the widest face I had ever seen on any kid. He had huge blond, curly hair, and he was one of those kids that you knew was mostly muscle, but covered with a few layers of fat. He was just a really big kid who, in fourth grade, had to wear the same size shirts as the ninth and tenth grade boys, and for some reason he stuck up for me a few times when people didn't want me on a team on the playground.

He wasn't the kind of kid anyone wanted to cross, and he was the boy you wanted on your dodge ball team. He was feared more than anything when he was on the opposing team. I usually ended up on his team, and would just stay behind him when he ran the line, and then I would come out from behind him to get someone out. It was like having a human shield.

The few times I was on a different dodge ball team than him, he ran the line and could have pulverized me, but instead hit the guy next to me. He never once took me out, and he could have knocked me right off of my feet as hard as he threw that ball.

Jimmy scowled, not willing to stand up to Farmers in any way, and went back to eating his PBJ. I couldn't have been more delighted to let Farmers pay me exactly forty cents more than I had paid. This lunch session was going well, and little did they know I had six more boxes of mini Atomic Fireballs in my lunch sack, as well as Lemonheads, jawbreakers, bubble gum balls, cinnamon toothpicks, Marathon bars, Black Cows, and Big Hunks.

Just then this really quiet kid named Salvatore, who had an accent like he was from somewhere else and was sitting four tables away, looked my way and started bobbing his head and wrinkling up his brow. Then his eyes grew huge and he nodded his head sideways frantically.

Sister Mary Claire was making her way around to our table too, shushing us, the 'noisy-boys' as the girls called us. I stuffed my lunch sack between my legs and tucked my shirt in around the bulge of candy, which was now hanging on my knees and hidden by the table as I pretended to be totally involved with my bologna sandwich.

"Mr. Peters, what are you up to?" she looked at me suspiciously.

"Eating my lunch," I said sullenly.

"And you, Mr. Farmers?"

He just shrugged and stared through her. Why would she single us out of two tables of boys? Then I saw the package of Atomic Fireballs in front of Farmers. I motioned with my eyes anxiously at him and Sister Mary Claire followed my gaze, catching Farmers as he tried to slide the box into his lunch sack.

Sister Mary Claire grabbed his lunch sack and poured the Atomic Fireballs out onto the table. The box opened, and little fireball bee bees went flying out over the table and rolled across the floor in about twenty different directions.

Sister Mary Claire pulled Farmers's ear and lifted him out of his seat with it. He followed her to Mother Superior's office.

As they left the lunchroom, Sister Mary Claire's back was to us, and she missed seeing thirty or so boys diving across the floor and stuffing the little Atomic bee bees into their mouths.

"Oh man, he is so dead!"

"Do you think he'll rat Peters out?"

My skin crawled at the thought. Farmers was a tough kid. He could take a paddling and keep his mouth shut. But would he do that for me?

"I'll bet he will tell Mother Superior about all of it. She is the best torturer around!"

"Yeah, he'll give it all up!"

"Oh yeah, he'll tell about the auction, the dare, even..."

"Peters sneaking across the street, all of it!"

"Oh man, Peters is more dead than Farmers!"

The murmuring grew and so did my fear of getting caught.

"Peters, you ought to just hand out all that candy and let us all hide it in our bags."

"Yeah, if you get caught with all that, man, you'll be dead."

Even though I knew the guys were just trying to get the candy for free, I thought it was probably a smart idea. I started to reach into my shirt when just then Sister Mary Claire came strolling back into the lunchroom with a very satisfied smirk on her face.

The whole lunchroom went dead quiet. That was when we all heard Farmers's cries of pain.

"STOP! NO! OW! I DIDN'T DO ANYTHING! WAHHH..."

The look of contentment on Sister Mary Claire's face was evil.

"Oh my gosh, he caved. Peters, you are so dead," someone I didn't even know whispered in my ear.

"Farmers is crying? I can't even believe that!" someone whispered at the other end of the table.I couldn't take any more. I was just about to stand up and admit my crime to Sister Mary Claire, hoping to possibly get some kind of a break for being honest about it, when out the window I saw Mother Superior pulling up in her long black car that she parked in the special spot closest to the building. But, if she was not even in her office and Farmers was screaming bloody murder, then who...?

I got it! And I nodded my head to the other guys when Sister Mary Claire's back was turned. All of a sudden, laughter rolled down my table, and soon everyone in the lunchroom was laughing and just cutting up. Everyone knew what was going on.

Sister Mary Claire stood up on one of the table benches and screamed, "STOP THAT THIS INSTANT! THERE WILL BE PEACE AND QUIET DURING MEALS HERE! DO YOU HEAR ME? STOP THAT INFERNAL LAUGHING!"***

The laughter died down, but the murmuring continued. After about five minutes Farmers walked into the lunchroom with really red eyes. He put on quite the show, grabbing his butt with both hands and walking with an exaggerated limp.

Sister Mary Claire looked at him with a smug look of satisfaction on her face that he had been brought to tears. "DO YOU SEE WHAT HAPPENS TO BAD BOYS WHO DON'T FOLLOW THE SCHOOL'S RULES?" she yelled, waving her hands in the air.

Farmers imitated her behind her back, making a hand gesture indicating a shaker of pepper.

Everyone cheered. I mean, the entire place went nuts! Even the lunch ladies were laughing.

Sister Mary Claire screamed, "WHAT ON EARTH? STOP THAT THIS INSTANT! EVERY SINGLE ONE OF YOU WHO ARE CLAPPING AND CHEERING WILL BE PUNISHED JUST LIKE FARMERS JUST WAS!"

Laughter broke out again. Catcalls came from the tables.

"EWWW, PLEASE, NOT ME!"

"OH NO, NOT LIKE FARMERS WAS!"

More laughter.

"I WANT SILENCE IN HERE! YOU THINK THIS IS A JOKE? YOU THINK IT IS FUNNY TO GET PUNISHED?" she screamed. She was now teetering on the bench spitting wildly when she talked.

When she wasn't looking his way, Farmers put his arms up in the air in a sign of victory and then pulled a huge black cow sucker out of his back pocket and kissed it, holding it up high.

"LOVE THAT MRS. WARD!" he mouthed for all to see.

There was whooping and hollering. The secret was still safe.

"YOU MUST SHUT UP!"

Sister Mary Claire could barely be heard over the loud roar in the lunchroom.

Someone whistled and then screamed really loud over the rest of the noise, "WHOA, HERE COMES MOTHER SUPERIOR! EVERYBODY DOWN!"

You could hear hundreds of people sitting instantly back in his or her places. Suddenly there was total silence.

Sister Mary Claire looked at everyone smugly (and ugly), as though she was the one who got it under control. "I AM WARN-ING YOU..."

"WHAT ON EARTH IS GOING ON HERE, SISTER MARY CLAIRE?" Mother Superior demanded, staring at Sister Mary Claire.

"These students are out of control and must be punished!"

Mother Superior peered over her cat-eye glasses, "IF YOU CAN-NOT HANDLE THESE STUDENTS, THEN..."

Sister Mary Claire looked like she might just collapse. "But I..."

"I will not have this discussion in front of the students. I would like to see you in my office in five minutes."

Mother Superior turned and started walking back toward her office. Sister Mary Claire meekly walked about two paces behind her.

"YEAH! GO GET HER!" Farmers stuck his arms up in the air, "GO GET HER, MOTHER SUPERIOR!"

Mother Superior whipped around, "You, young man, will come to my office in ten minutes."

"Yes, mam," Farmers said in the smallest voice I have ever heard him use.

Mother Superior and Sister Mary Claire walked out of the lunchroom and down the hall toward Mother Superior's office. Mother Superior's voice echoed from the hallway through the quiet lunchroom, "Mrs. Sampson, please take over the lunchroom duty. Sister Mary Claire and I have some discussing to do."

When Mrs. Sampson, the nicest teacher ever at St. Joe's, walked in, the whole lunchroom broke out in applause and then a chant moved through the lunchroom, "MRS. SAMPSON! MRS. SAMP-SON!"

With a huge smile on her face she spoke out, "Okay, you lovely children, you must quiet down now, please. You don't want to get me in trouble now, do you?" she giggled in a way that let us all know she was with us completely. "I wouldn't want to get any pepper in my eye!" she winked at Farmers.

I yelled, "I love you, Mrs. Sampson! You're the best!"

The entire lunchroom went totally dead quiet. I was so embarrassed. I stood there, knowing my face was growing red, and I simply couldn't move. Yelling out your love for a teacher could go beyond ridicule.

All of a sudden Farmers yelled, "I love you too, Mrs. Sampson!"

A fifth grade girl yelled, "You are the best!"

Then another student yelled a compliment, then another and another. It was clear that Mrs. Sampson was by far the most popular teacher, and then the chant started again with gusto, "MRS. SAMPSON! MRS. SAMPSON! MRS. SAMPSON! MRS. SAMPSON! MRS. SAMPSON!"

My hands stopped feeling so clammy. I wasn't embarrassed by my outburst anymore. I was actually kind of proud of myself. Everyone was joining in, and I was afraid Mother Superior was going to come back if the noise level didn't drop.

Mrs. Sampson had tears in her eyes, and pleaded with us to be quiet, and everyone did quiet down after a bit. She walked over to my table and whispered, "I love you, too, Gabriel. Now, you better find a place to put all of that before you get in some trouble." She motioned toward the huge bulk hiding under my shirt.

She started walking around and talking to groups at their tables now back to eating lunch. Then she called back to me, "I would suggest your stomachs!"

She started to laugh, and then was greeted with big hugs from the girls two tables over.

I nodded and then asked Farmers, "What happened?"

191

Farmers leaned over and whispered in my ear, "Sister Ann Martin, that's what happened. The old pepper trick. But now I have to go see the real deal. Mother Superior is going to kill me."

Every so often someone would start chanting "MRS. SAMPSON!" and others would join in again. Mrs. Sampson kept trying to get control of the lunchroom but it wasn't working very well. Everyone was just too keyed up now with all the commotion.

Just then Sister Ann Martin walked in. A sudden hush rushed over the lunchroom. "Hello, students. If you would please bring the noise level down a few notches, you will sure make my day a little easier. Mother Superior is trying to talk to one of the teachers, and the noise coming from the lunchroom is quite loud. And I believe Mother Superior is planning on being here the remainder of the day, so discipline, I am afraid, is going to be administered by her alone."

She winked at the boys at my table.

Nods and "okay, we wills" and "sorry" filled the lunchroom.

Then Sister Ann Martin looked at my table again and started motioning with her finger, "Mr. Farmers, will you come with me, please. Mother Superior has asked me to attend to one immediate disciplinary matter because she will be detained a bit longer with her current conversation than she had expected."

A huge smile came over Franklin Ferdinand Farmers's huge, red face. He held his hand up for me to give him five, and when he returned the five I thought my hand might never stop stinging.

"Good luck, Farmers!" I said.

Everyone started laughing.

Someone called out, "Yeah, you need some salt?"

"Oh, they do go together don't they?"

"You are such a baaaad boy, Franky Farmers!" and other taunts filled the lunchroom until both Mrs. Sampson and Sister Ann Martin put their fingers to their mouth and shushed us.

Mrs. Sampson looked curious, but somehow I knew she knew what was up. She stood on the other side of the lunchroom with the two lunch ladies while everyone finished their lunches, no doubt talking about what had just happened. Every so often she would look over to where I was holding the quietest auction ever and would wink at me when our eyes met.

By the end of lunch I had made a profit of six dollars and thirty-two cents. I had let Johnny Germain win some Lemonheads with a thirty-two cent bid, even though he said he had forty cents, which it turned out he didn't. Now I could go up the bait shop and really get some good wholesale deals. I told all the boys to break out their piggy banks the next Friday, because I was probably going to be crossing the street again and the auction was going to be H-O-T!

I gave Mrs. Sampson a Marathon bar, because she once told me that caramel was her favorite, and a Marathon bar was basically caramel covered with sweet chocolate. I saved out one box of Lemonheads and a handful of bubble gum, which I put in Amy's desk with a note when I got back to class, but what that note said is forever going to be a secret!

Turns out, for the rest of the day we had a substitute teacher, because as was explained to us, Sister Mary Claire felt ill and needed to return to the convent to relax. Even while Sister Ann Martin was explaining it to us she was giggling.

I thought to myself how glad I was that God had at least one really nice wife.

CHAPTER TWENTY-THREE

Field Day

I woke up with a strange feeling in my stomach. Somehow I just knew something big was about to happen, and I wasn't sure if it was going to be good or bad. I couldn't shake the feeling, and answered all of Mom's and Dad's questions with "Uh huh" and "hmmm."

When I got to school there were posters on all of the walls, announcing the most thrilling upcoming event. The whole school was buzzing with excitement. Kids from all grades were running down the hall yelling and screaming, they were all so anxious and eager for it to get here.

Man, nothing could be further from how I felt. Springtime is mostly fun, but it looks like one of the big traditions that I wasn't looking forward to was going to be here - Field Day.

"This year, I'm going to win the 100-yard dash!" a seventh grader yelled to his buddies.

"Nah, no one can beat Scott Rogers!"

"Did you hear about that new kid in fifth grade from Minneapolis? He is some kind of Superkid. He can run as fast as a ninth grader!"

"Yeah, the kid with the wire-rimmed glasses? He's a major fox," one of the girls said.

Hmm... I wondered what it would be like to have people talk about me that way.

I also envied anyone who had wire-rimmed glasses instead of the big, black goggles that passed as glasses still on my own nose. Mom had said if I took better care of my glasses I could get some of the wire frames, but within the week I had broken yet another pair, putting off the possibility again.

Wire frames are so expensive, and we have had to get now three frames already, since one of them got snapped right in half when Kevin hit me in the face with a ball, another one broke when I sat on them and my last pair sunk to the bottom of the lake I wasn't supposed to be near at night, so I couldn't ask for help to try to fish them off the bottom before they got lost. I'm a klutz, I probably won't ever get wire-rimmed glasses.

I had always dreaded Field Day as much as most people were excited about it. I pray for rain! Our Father, who art in heaven, bring us mucho rain, to spoil the day, would be okay, then I won't run a lane...

It was exactly one month until the big event, and one month away from the first day of spring. All of our gym classes would be dedicated to sprinting, running and jumping, reminding me on a daily basis of how far I fall short of normal.

Last year against Sister Mary Claire's wishes, Mrs. Sampson let me sit out of the events and gave me some cool jobs, like holding the tape at the end of the sprints so the fastest kid could lean into it just like they do in the Olympics. There is NO WAY the mean Sister Mary Claire is going to let me off this year. She doesn't like me a single bit, and I don't think she likes Mrs. Sampson much either!

I read the signs, dreaming of what it must be like for Scott Rogers, Quinton Johnsen and Mike Whitley to know that they had it in the bag already. Those three are as fast as the wind, and no one would beat them, not from St. Joseph's or any other school.

As hard as it is for me to admit it, I resent them, even though they are always nice to me in the hall. Well, I really just resent the fact that I won't ever be able to know what it feels like to run that fast.

Man, what it would be like to walk up and down the hall with all of the younger kids "oohing" and "ahhing" because you were so cool? The school heroes! Soon signs will pop up on the walls with their names, events and their anticipated times from gym class trials, to get everyone excited.

But truth is, even though I dream every day of being the one picked first for kickball or the one all the kids will pull for to win the annual Field Day events, I would trade it all to simply be able to walk without bobbing like one of those blow-up clowns you see at birthday parties - the ones filled with sand at the bottom, and all the kids punching it to get it to bop back up. That's me, Punching-Clown-Gabriel. Sure, my leg has grown out quite a bit, but I still hobble when I try to run too fast.

I then imagined myself running in the races really fast, so that I left all of the other runners in my dust. What everyone else would see though was me, slightly limping along in the far lane, me and Franky Farmers - the slowest boy - beaten even by Emily, the slowest girl in fourth grade.

Everyone has to participate this year. I won't be getting out of being there unless my prayer is answered.

Sister Mary Claire walked up and twisted my arm harder than necessary. "GABRIEL PETERS, WHERE'RE YOU SUP-POSED TO BE?"

I hurried down the hall, imagining myself running fast "like a rabbit" across the large schoolyard, excited and happy and WIN-NING. I saw myself someday sprinting across the playground.

When I was out of earshot of Sister Mary Claire I whispered loudly; "Faster than a speeding bullet, able to leap tall batwomen in a single bound... For Gabriel Peters the crowd does sound! Then he tosses the evil batwoman over the fence! Now the crowds happy, no longer tense!"

All of the boys ran in one big mob to the kickball diamond. The girls were jumping rope and having a blast. I noticed Felicia Finkleschmidt huddled against the monkey bars, rocking herself against it like she does every day, with none of the other girls ever talking to her.

Felicia is plump and wears pink, sparkly cat-eye glasses*. 'Plump' is my mom's nice way of referring to a person who stretch-es the seams of her clothing more than everyone else.

Felicia picks her nose, and in Geography class I watched her eat it too, gross, totally gross. Still, she seems like a nice person, and she is lonely like I was last year.

I feel sorry for her, but whenever I try to talk to her she is sort of rude to me. I think she expects anyone who talks to her to be mean to her. I have seen some of the girls act like they are her friend and then trick her. But Felicia doesn't care what anyone thinks of her. She has said so many times.

One time when some rude boys were making fun of her on the playground she just responded with, "STICKS AND STONES MAY BREAK MY BONES, BUT NAMES WILL NEVER HURT ME..."

Now everyone has heard that - that isn't so original or witty

*cat-eye glasses - popular style in the 60s and 70s, mostly cool when white and on a mom, not a Batwoman! If a Batwoman wore them, they should be black, and be called 'bat-eye glasses!'

- but she always follows it up with a new second line that I am certain she made up herself: "YOU ARE MEAN, I AM NOT, I'LL BE REMEMBERED, YOU'LL BE FORGOT!"

On the day they were calling her really mean names, especially this one totally obnoxious boy named Michael Arbinari, Sister Anne Margaret, the art teacher, left the room to find some paste, and Felicia stood on her chair and said; "STICKS AND STONES, MAY BREAK MY BONES, BUT NAMES WILL NEVER HURT ME. I AM SMART AND YOU ARE DUMB, SOMEDAY I'LL BE FAMOUS, AND YOU'LL BE A BUM!"

That one just cracked me up. If a boy had said it, the mean jerk Michael Arbinari, would have punched him, but to punch a girl makes you a sissy and he wouldn't do that.

It was fun to see a girl put him in his place. He just stood there with his stupid, ugly mouth hanging open, his face all red like he was really mad, but I think he was embarrassed to be shut down by a girl.

Then several of the boys started to make fun of him.

"Hey Michael, you gonna let a girl push you round?"

"Michael is a chicken, scared of a girl!" another sneered.

Michael's face turned all red and he stepped toward Felicia. "Shut up, you stupid girl. You will never be famous. You are just plain ugly."

Felicia stepped off her chair and came toward him. She towered over him by about a foot.

"Take it back, Michael Arbinari!" she shouted.

"I won't, UGLY face!"

He barely got the words out of his mouth when she doubled

up her fist and punched him square in the mouth, sending him crashing backwards into a bunch of chairs, and before he could even sit up she jumped on top of him and started to wail on him like a crazy person. She was slapping his face and banging his head against the ground, shouting something that sounded like a wild Indian.

Everyone was gathered around to see this most incredible scene, but soon several of the Batwomen came running in to see what the commotion was all about and broke up the fight. Michael Arbinari was screaming and crying to get her off of him. He had a bloody nose and the beginning of a major shiner on his eye that mostly kept his mouth shut after that.

An announcer comes on for all to hear; "Superstar kickball star, GABRIEL PETERS! He's on home plate, the ball is rolling in, he sees it, he kicks, it clears the fence, it clears the house, another house, and lands in the backyard where Michael Arbinari goes to retrieve it. A huge Doberman Pinscher bites Michael right on the butt. The giant dog is dragging him all over the yard and he is muddy and crying; the kids begin to point at him and laugh. He wets his pants. His parents decide to send him to a reform school where big bullies decide he is the one to pick on, and every day he gets ten thousand spit yoyos and five thousand atomic wedgies. No one at St. Joseph's School ever sees Michael Arbinari, the world's biggest bully, again!! Then everyone gathers around cheering. Gabriel Peters has won the game! Felicia Finkleschmidt throws the disc farther than any boy ever has, and Farmers throws his arm around her, and no one is ever mean to her again! They lift Gabriel on their shoulders and carry him around the schoolyard chanting, "GABRIEL'S NUMBER ONE! GABRIEL'S NUMBER ONE! GABRIEL'S NUMBER ONE!"

Suddenly a voice jarred me out of my daydream. What I was actually doing was limping as fast as I could along a hedge I had found at the back of the schoolyard, where I could hide from the little gang of boys who found great joy in making the fourth graders

days miserable. They were of course led by the biggest jerk in the fifth grade, Michael Arbinari.

It is amazing how every class has a bully. Last year this kid named Ronnie was the bully everyone had to run away from, but he kind of turned out to be kind of nice to me by the end of the year. But this kid, Michael Arbinari, is just a total, nasty jerk.

Well, school is going to be out soon, and he doesn't really pick on me much anyway, especially now, because Farmers and Felicia and I eat lunch together, and when Arbinari walks by Felicia growls at him and he runs off like a sissy.

My prayer wasn't answered. There wasn't a cloud in the sky on Field Day. I got into a relay team with four boys from my class. We placed second!

Then I had to run a 200-yard dash and I finished fourth. That was out of eight kids, but I wasn't in last place anymore! Then we had to do the long jump, and I couldn't believe it. On account of all of the physical therapy I did because of my leg, I was actually able to jump longer than anyone else in the whole fourth grade! Some of the boys accused me of cheating, so Sister Mary Dumbhead Claire made me do it again.

This time I had an audience and I sailed through the air. I actually gained two inches on my other jump, and set a record for fourth graders at Field Day.

Mrs. Sampson was there cheering me on and gave me a big hug. "I am so proud of you, Gabriel!"

When I got my blue ribbon Amy kissed me on the cheek, and told me that I was her hero. That made me decide to get some running shoes. I think maybe I will be a world-famous track star when I grow up, just like all of those guys who run in the Olympics.

I have never set a record in anything in my whole life, until this year's Field Day, that is.

Amy and I made a plan to go to the sweet shop with Farmers and Felicia on Saturday, and then to the movie matinee. Maybe I would even see if Carl and Denise could go. After all, Carl was a lot nicer to me when Denise was around.

CHAPTER TWENTY-FOUR

Verb Schmerb

Today was the worst day of the whole year in class. There's only ten more days of school. I just hope I can hold on that long. Sister Mary Claire is the meanest person I've ever met in my entire life. Her breath smells like broccoli. Today she was terrible to me.

She made fun of me in front of the whole class because I couldn't answer a simple English question about a verb. I left my glasses in the nurse's office, and Sister Mary Dumbhead wouldn't let me go and get them. So I tried to read the board to see which word was the verb in the sentence, but it was so fuzzy, it just didn't make any sense to me, and she wouldn't read it out loud for me.

I have to <u>write</u> the sentence out fifty times as my homework assignment, "The boy <u>pumped</u> his fist in the air at the train conductor," and underline the verb in EVERY sentence. How ridiculous is that? In my neighborhood the irrigation water <u>flows</u> from the pump, the pump is actually a machine that <u>pumps</u> water and we call the pond the 'pump,' too, so 'pump' isn't always a verb, it is a noun, which is a person, place, or thing, not an action, and the pump, which is actually a pond that everyone in my neighborhood <u>calls</u> the pump, is a place where I <u>hunt</u> crawdads and frogs, so <u>hunt</u> is the verb in that sentence.

The point is that I <u>know</u> the difference between a verb and a noun, maybe better than the Batwoman Sister Mary Dumbhead Claire does, I just can't <u>see</u> it when it is written up on the board from the back of the room where she makes me <u>sit</u> without my glasses so I can't <u>see</u>!

Sister Mary Claire <u>wears</u> thick, cat-eye glasses, which she <u>peers</u> and <u>glares</u> and <u>scowls</u> over with a puckered-up, ugly-as-sin raisin-pinched face (I could get in trouble for <u>writing</u> that). She always, always looked angry about something, and I was scared to death of her from the first moment I <u>met</u> her (note that I underlined all of the verbs. That is called sarcasm*).

"Gabriel Peters, for a boy <u>named</u> after an angel** and an apostle, you sure are a handful!" She would <u>say</u> things like that to me all the time.

I couldn't help it that my name <u>reads</u> like a Bible story, and man oh man, those angels are quite a handful, too. Like that angel that <u>slips</u> into Mary's room and <u>tells</u> her she is going to be a mom, or the time the angel <u>tells</u> Joseph that is okay to be Jesus' father and all. Sheesh, Sister Mary Claire doesn't even know the most popular of all Bible stories if she doesn't <u>think</u> an angel is a handful!

Okay, I am tired of <u>underlining</u> verbs, and I think I made my point after all.

Truth is, Sister Mary Claire doesn't really like anyone, 'cept sometimes the girls. She is grouchy and overall just a not very nice

*sarcasm (noun), the use of irony to mock or convey contempt ** Gabriel (in the Bible), the archangel who foretold the birth of Jesus to the Virgin Mary (Luke 1:26-38), and who also appeared to Zacharias, father of John the Baptist.

person. I always thought God's son would have one really nice wife, but they keep saying all of the Sisters at my school are married to God. No way!

I asked my Dad about that, and he just said he didn't understand why God would want multiple wives, that one wife is a handful enough. He also told me not to tell my mom he said that for two reasons, 1. Dad is not a Catholic like Mom, and, 2. It wouldn't be good if Mom heard dad was calling her a 'handful.' I wonder why He wants so many wives when my dad says keeping up with one wife is a full-time job.

So when I said bad things about Sister Mary Claire in my diary, I could just hear what Mom would say; "If you don't have anything nice to say, don't say anything at all." Well, I'm not saying it, I'm writing it, and it's my diary anyhow. Sister Mary Claire IS A JERK! Sister Mary Claire SHOULD HAVE MARRIED OLD MAN STOLTZ INSTEAD OF GOD SO THEY COULD BE TOTAL JERKS TOGETHER!

Speaking of diaries, the diary Mom bought me is real leather. It says so right in the front, "Genuine Cowhide," and it's dyed burgundy-red. She said, "You have so many things going on in your mind all the time that I thought it would help you to work things out to write about them. You are a good storyteller. Maybe if you write down your ideas it will focus your writing and your thoughts. No one is allowed to read your private diary unless you say so, and that is why it has a lock and key."

"Not even you, Mom?"

"Not even me."

So I wrote, Sister Mary Claire IS A JERK! SHE HAS NO HAIR UNDER HER STUPID BLACK BAT-HAT, THAT'S WHY NO ONE WANTED TO MARRY HER EXCEPT GOD'S SON, CUZ HE IS NICE AND SEES PAST UGLY, MEAN JERKS!

I wonder if even Jesus isn't allowed to read my diary. I hope not. He might get mad if I say bad things about one of his wives.

The diary has an attached leather bookmark to keep my place because there are no dates to make you write every day in order, which I think is a smart idea since you mostly write on the days when things have happened that are important enough to write about, right?

Also, do boys keep diaries? I'm just asking because my brother Carl told me only sissies and girls have diaries. I have to hide the diary too, because Carl likes to snoop in my room, even if Mom says he can't read it, or maybe especially because she says that.

Mom bought the diary for me just last year. But it feels like it was a million and two years ago, on account of the fact that in that past year my legs started growing at a totally different pace, and my eyes are all shot and I had to get glasses, and I got beat up and tripped and pushed around hundreds of times by a bully and his bully friends. How embarrassing is that? Boy-oh-boy, when you have something that makes you stand out, or in my case, stand crooked, the other boys really don't like you much at all.

One group of boys who made fun of everyone would usually treat me with the same, lame insults whenever they saw me out of earshot of one of the teachers. Their favorite stupid joke that they used to say over and over to me on the playground goes, 'What do you call a woman with a short leg? ILENE! Get it, I LEAN?'

That is so dumb. I mean, I am a boy and they tell me a stupid short leg girl joke. I just always acted like I didn't hear them.

Then one day, after his friend had said the Ilene joke for the millionth time, one of them said, "Hey guys, what do you call a boy with a short leg? IGABE! Get it? I GABE?" They all thought that was so funny.

Mom kept telling me that I am something special. That always comes up when she was working on my cuts and bruises from being picked on. She told me that if those boys knew the real me, they would think I was the greatest kid in the world.

THEY DID NOT THINK THAT! THEY HATED ME! THEY WERE JERKS! JERKS! JERKS!

Okay, I just had to get that all out somewhere where no one else would ever read it! Things are a lot better for me this year, and it all started because I made the bullies laugh - and scared a few, too. So maybe if I am such a good storyteller like Dad says, Mom getting me this book to write in is a good idea.

I never wrote in the diary at all last year when things were going so bad, not one word that is, if you don't count my cursive name on the inside cover, Gabriel Peters, which I wrote on it with Mom watching me just to prove to her that I really did like it.

I guess my face that Christmas morning must have gone all scrunched when I opened the package with the diary in it, because Mom must have asked me a zillion and one times if I liked it. She told me if I didn't like it she would take me to the mall to exchange it for something I really liked. But, it was in a Hallmark box, and all they have there are smelly candles and syrupy greeting cards for all that dorky Valentine's Day stuff, all the kissy-kissy feelings that I don't understand or care about anyhow. What would a kid my age get in exchange there?

Besides, it is not polite to exchange a gift that someone took the time to pick out just right for you. Especially if they live with you, cuz then every time you aren't writing in your diary, they know you took it back.

Maybe the fact that my brother was opening a really cool Hot Wheels track at the time and I had already opened two books and now a diary had something to do with my lack of excitement.

Little did I know that the diary could have seen me through my baddest times last year if I had just used it.

I know 'baddest' isn't a real word, but it sure is better than the real ones. Someday I want to write my own dictionary, full of the words I like to use that make more sense than some of the ones we use. For instance, 'baddest' instead of 'worst.' My mom makes liverwurst sandwiches' and sometimes puts them in my lunch - there's that word 'worst.' Now, I really like liverwurst sandwiches, especially with lots of mustard, but when you combine 'liver' and 'worst' in a name of lunchmeat you are bound to gross someone out. 'Worst' is a bad word, 'liverbest' sandwich sounds dorky, so maybe it could be called 'bolognagood' sandwiches. Everyone loves bologna, right? The other thing about 'baddest' is some people, mostly teenagers, use it when they really mean 'goodest,' like 'That is the baddest Corvette I've ever seen,' which means they think it is the bestest, not the worstest - confusing eh?

Still, I felt bad that Mom never saw me writing in the diary for a whole year. For a long time it seemed too good to mess up with my silly thoughts, ones that I figured wouldn't amount to a hill of beans anyway. So what I should have been doing all that time is writing my own dictionary of words, then she would have seen me writing something and she would have thought I was dealing with all of my feelings like she always wants me to. So here are some words that I wrote in my diary to add to my someday dictionary (by the way, I moved to the living room where Mom is sitting so she could see me writing in the diary).

Baddest - *a better word for 'worst'* **Bully** - *people who should never get to be mean again, and should have someone like them, only bigger and badder, to pick on them.* **Badder** - *worse than 'bad,' or just short of 'baddest'*

See what I mean? My dictionary makes sense, cuz that is how people talk. I thought it would be better to wait to write in the diary until when I had some real stories to write about. Who knows maybe someday I would write a book, but that would have to wait. But who wants to hear some boring stories about some boring fourth-grade repeater who doesn't know all that much, anyway? Besides, I didn't have anything going on that ANYONE wanted to hear about. Most people just want ACTION, not just the day in the life of some four-eyed dork, who actually might be Private Eye Dirk The Smirk. The detective stuff is what they want.

I am going to begin to write about the action, action, action now, and maybe I will make Sister Mary Claire underline all of my verbs which should be a million since it is an action book.

Every time I try to tell a story at the dinner table, my big brother would start making big yawning noises, and under his breath (actually only kind of under his breath), he would say things like, "Annnnnd your point issss?" and "And we care about this dumb story becaaaause?" Then he would hold his hands up to his eyes as if he had to keep them open with his fingers and thumbs.

Mom would scowl at his rudeness, "Be nice, Carl! Get your elbows off of the table PLEASE!"

And that would be the end of his discipline session. It would last all of ten seconds, and then he would kick me under the table or something like that to show me he was in charge.

I swear my big brother Carl gets away with murder, all because he has a "learning disability." Carl is a seventh grader who should be in eighth, but he got held back because of his "learning disability." I think he fakes most of it anyway, because he gets all the attention. Sheesh, he gets away with murder, I tell you.

He gets held back, I get pushed forward, then I get held back... this is the weirdest family in the history of families.

CHAPTER TWENTY-FIVE

Zombie Boogers

Saturday morning, Andy and I dug night crawlers* out of Dad's vegetable garden, in a contest to see who could get the longest one. Andy won. I never win at anything, except I did win at Field Day, and really I won big, so I don't mind it when it's Andy who wins, because he doesn't get to win many more times than I do with all of his big brothers.

All of a sudden an excitement welled up in me that I couldn't hold back.

"ANDY, CAN YOU BELIEVE WE ARE ALMOST OUT OF SCHOOL?"

"Yeah, this is g-g-going to be the b-b-best summer ever d-dude!"

"Yeah! Hey by the way, I'M ALMOST OFFICIALLY A FIFTH GRADER!! FINALLY!"

I felt so excited to think that we had three months of summer adventure coming. Rumors around the neighborhood were starting to heat up about this old lady who lives up on a hill in a haunted house. I wondered if it might end up in a dare-off that

*night crawler (noun), an earthworm, in particular one that comes to the surface at night and is collected for use as fishing bait.

209

someone would have to go up there to touch her house or something. It made my skin feel cold just thinking about it, and it was a really warm morning.

Andy pulled on the end of the night crawler, who was trying to get back into its hole. It stretched about ten feet long, and then kind of popped out just like they do when momma robins pull on them.

Andy thwacked me on the arm with that big worm, leaving a slimy mark on me.

"Hey, you Twit!" I yelled.

He started to laugh out loud, harder than before. "HEY G-GABE! CHECK THIS ONE OUT! Th-this old n-n-night crawler's like a long, s-skinny FLESH C-C-COATED ZOMBIE BOOGER!"

He started laughing so hard at his own joke that he fell down to his knees. Then he shoved a night crawler in his nostril and let it hang there and made these funny zombie grunts and moans and held his hand up and out in front like he was the walking dead, "ARGHHHHHH, I M-MUST EAT, G-G-GABRIEL, I M-MUST EAT THE UGLY B-B-BOY!"

"Yeah, you should know about zombie boogers, you nose-picking zombie!" I thumped his arm hard and tried to dodge out of reach.

"Yeah r-r-ight, me, wh-what about you?" He punched me back on the shoulder.

I held a worm up to my nose and started walking around like Andy-The-Zombie-Booger-Boy.

"I AM ANDY, THE FIVE-FOOT-EIGHT-INCH BOOGER BOY... ARGHHHH MUST EAT MORE BOOGER BRAINS..." I dangled the worm in a U-shape so it looked like it was hanging out of both of my nostrils.

That's how it always is with us. We talk about stuff that makes my mom roll her eyes. I mean, you tell me, is there much stuff funnier than boogers made out of slimy worms?

All of a sudden Andy shoved his hand at my face and the night crawler got smooshed up inside one of my nostrils. "AHHH-HGHHH, you idiot butthead, it's up inside my brain!"

Andy started to talk in a spooky voice, "That w-was the d-d-day the zombie w-worm took over G-Gabe's pea-sized brain."

"I'm serious, you big dummy, why'd you do that? YECH!"

The cold, wet worm was stuck up way inside my nostril, and it felt so disgusting, like when you go to a Halloween party and they have a 'bowl of brains' which is always just oil-slimed spaghetti that you are supposed to feel with a blindfold on, only this was up inside my head, not on my hands.

I did a farmer's blow right toward Andy and then started running at him, "You jerk! I'm gonna kill you!"

I started chasing Andy around the garden, blowing worm guts at him with another farmer's blow from each nostril and trying to catch him so I could whip my snot-slimed-worm on his shirt. By the time I caught up with him, he was across the gravel road under the tree house laughing really hard and trying to climb

211

up the tree, but his feet were too muddy from the garden.

"You are soooooo dead, dude!" I yelled.

"Oh yeah, I'm s-s-o sc-scared..."

"You sound like it! I mean, you're stuttering and all... "

Andy whipped around and looked at me. My eyes must have grown twice their size as I realized I had just stepped over the line by making fun of his stuttering. "H-Hey, I didn't mean..."

Andy raised his eyebrow at my stutter, and then all of a sudden we both just started cracking up. That's the coolest thing about best friends; you can say things to each other no one else can and get away with it.

"Are we going fishing or what?" I said nervously, trying to change the subject.

"You're the one ch-chasing me around, d-dorky boy worm b-brain!"

"'D-D-Dorky boy?' Is that all you have?"

We laughed so hard tears rolled down my cheeks.

"'Worm b-brain?'"

"W-Watch out, you're g-gonna m-m-make me spitting m-mad like Old M-Man Stoltz!"

Andy laughed so suddenly that a big stream of spit flew out of his mouth.

I laughed pretty hard at that one, remembering the time we had all tangled up on our bikes because of Mr. Stoltz. "Whatever, zombie butt, I'm so going to get you back for the worm squish!"

"Oooh... you are s-so tough!"

"Oh, you ain't seen nothing yet!" I gave him my best double bicep pose, which looked like I was straightening up two large rubber bands.

We went on and on like that as we walked down to the lake to try to catch the famous Carp Monster.

Later as Andy was trying to get around this small cotton-wood tree where you can see straight down into the crystal-clear water of the lake and watch the bluegills and sunfish swimming, I pushed him really hard and he went flying down the embankment, landing right in the lake. "Told you I'd get you back!"

I ran back up the embankment laughing so hard I thought my sides would explode.

Andy came flying out of the water screaming, "Peters you're a d-d-dead m-man!"

He came up the embankment with a purpose, but he was so wet he lost his footing and slid back down into the water. He tried it again and slid back down again. Then he started walking along the shallows until he could get to a flatter part, but by that time I was already running behind the trees along the path that led around the lake to the stream where it flowed out toward the bull snake field.

Then I doubled back and ran right past him, where he was twisting the water out of his t-shirt. "Not if you can't catch me!"

I ran down the side of the lake and ducked under the sand-stone cliff. This really weird eerie crying sound was coming down the hill. I looked up and realized that it was coming from that crazy old lady's house.

Chills ran down my spine. I looked around at Andy and he must have had the same terror on his face that I had on mine because his eyes got really big. I took off running along the bottom of the cliff, hidden by some tall bushes. I knew somehow that her house was going to be a part of a dare-off coming up, and I wanted to be anywhere but there in case I got picked out for it.

Andy crept inside the small cave where I had pushed my body in, trying to hide.

"Wh-What w-w-was th-that?"

"DUDE, THAT'S THAT OLD LADY WHO ATE THAT KID ONE TIME," I whispered, maybe too loud. "Remember that night when we were all roasting wieners and marshmallows down here, and we heard that?"

All of sudden the eerie wailing got louder and she came around from the back of her house. She was wandering in her front yard, her dress blowing behind her and her long, wild hair standing straight up. Then she looked right at us and we both screamed and pushed our bodies back into the back of the cave as much as we could, all the time watching up the hill, ready to escape if she were to start heading down there.

Andy and I waited for what seemed like forever for her to go back to her backyard, then we sneaked out of the cave, huddled close to the cliffs and escaped through the ditch. We didn't even take our tackle box or fishing poles. We just had to get out of there fast.

We ran all the way up the gravel hill road, cutting over to Venus Avenue through Mr. Patchett's yard to avoid getting too close to the crazy old lady's house.

We climbed up into the tree house and spied on her with the binoculars as she was working in her huge garden. There is a giant gargoyle* right in the center, and it looks like it is going to come alive under a full moon some night and go out to capture vic-

*gargoyle (noun), a grotesque carved human or animal face or figure projecting from the gutter of a building, typically acting as a spout to carry water clear of a wall.

tims for the crazy old lady. Every so often the crazy old lady would turn around and look right toward the tree house, like she knew somehow we were up there spying on her. It made my skin crawl.

But, somehow being that close to my house made me feel safer, so we started talking about other stuff to take our minds off how scary shewas, even in the daytime.

We decided we needed to call a special meeting of the Secret Brotherhood of Boys to figure out what we were going to do about that crazy old lady. One by one the guys showed up and crawled up the side of the tree into the tree house, where we all watched the old lady wandering around in her yard.

Andy said, "Maybe T-Tony could g-g-gas her out of the n-neighborhood.

"WHAT?" Tony scowled.

"W-WELL, YOU D-DO HAVE MORE G-G-GAS THAN ANYONE ELSE ALIVE!" Andy started talking about some of the funny things that happened at the last meeting. Sometimes when the Secret Brotherhood of Boys meets in the tree house or our underground fort, Tony thinks it's funny to practically blow the lid off the underground dirt fort with his gas, and man we all scramble out of there as fast as we can. It is SO BAD you think you are gonna die down there! 'Mustard Gas Tony' we call him now, or just 'MG.' I mean, he sounds like a dad-sized guy when he rips one. All of us fall down in hysterics when he does that.

One time all of us guys in the Secret Brotherhood were having a top-secret spy meeting in the tree house by the pond across the street from my house, when Tony pushed his butt right down on the floor of the tree house and pushed out a huge one that rumbled right through the tree house floor. We were laughing so hard that Butch rolled right out of the tree house, landing in the pond. It was a good thing the pond was full. Man, that cracked us up, but

I wasn't sure which was funnier, Tony and his amazing gas or Butch tumbling out of the tree house and screaming like a kindergarten girl all the way down as he fell.

Butch stood down there covered in muddy water, looking like my brother does right when he wakes up in the morning if I scare him awake, which I try to do as often as possible. I thought Butch was gonna cry, but he just stood there in the water looking all stunned and then started to laugh again and dove underwater, jumping around and just having a great old time. One by one we swung out of the tree house and let go, splashing down into the pond, practically landing on each other and doing our cannonballs and jackknife dives screaming, "COWABUNGA" and "LOOOOOOOK OUUUT BELOWWWW!"

Two days earlier we had seen this ten-foot long bull snake*** in the pond, and not one of us had gone in for a swim since, but when Butch started screaming and yelling and splashing that water looked mighty good and we all lost our heads. Right as I was splashing down and Butch was coming up out of the water, the guys up still in the tree house started yelling, "Butch, watch out, the king bull snake is headed right at you!"

The funny thing is that the side of the pond right under the tree house has the steepest bank. It is muddy and full of holes on account of the fact that the crawdads and frogs live there.

Butch tried to climb up the bank, and kept slipping back down into the muddy water. Me and Craig knew the guys were kidding because Murph, the only kid there with black camouflage paint on his face yelling about the bull snake, was swinging down into the pond and there was no way he would do that if the king bull snake was really there. We were all laughing and yelling so hard when the most awful thing happened.

Butch was screaming and scrambling to try to get out of the

***bull snake - a constrictor found commonly on the plains and prairies of N. America.

water, and he must have scared that king bull snake awake, cause sure enough it had been sunning itself right on top of that muddy bank in the grass, where no one could see it. Now, even though Tony, Andy and Johnny said they had seen it for real, I know none of us had seen it that day when we were just trying to scare Butch.

That fat old snake swam right into the water toward Butch. I swam hard and hustled out the front gate as fast as I could, running back to the tree and climbing up into the tree house where that snake couldn't go. It was a good thing that Butch was up to his belly in water because when he saw that huge snake heading toward him he peed in his pants (I only know this because Butch told me in secret later). Man-o-man, if the guys would have known that he never would have lived it down, but I am really good at keeping secrets, wink-wink, nudge-nudge.

The bull snake swam across the surface of the pond and slithered out where we could see it from the tree house. Later, it was sunning itself up on some rocks and not paying any attention to Butch at all, and from this angle we could see that it wasn't that big after all, maybe four feet long, which is still a good size, but I catch four footers all the time, and they aren't scary at all, so there was no way that snake was the king bull snake.

So because it was so hot and the water still looked so fun, we all took turns swinging off the rope swing and splashing down, trying to land on top of Butch. Murph stayed in the tree house as our lookout, in case that bull snake on the rocks was just the baby and HUGE MOMMA snake showed up, but she would have to be like fifty feet long if she were that snake's momma. Murph kept talking into his thumb like he had an army walkie-talkie and was communicating with some intelligence person on the other end.

Right about the time we all forgot about the snake, Murph starts screaming at the top of his lungs from up in the tree house, "SNAKE!THEMOTHEROFALLBULLSNAKESISSLIDINGIN-

TOTHEPONDRIGHTATCHA!MANTHEBATTLESTATIONS!
SUBMARINERSDEPLOY!PILOTS,GETREADY-
FORTHEDEPTH CHARGES!"

"Depth charge? What the heck is a depth charge, War Boy?"
Butch growled.

"DUH,whodoesn'tknowwhatadepthchargeis,youidiot?Everyone
knowsit'sanexplosivechargedroppedfromashiporairplanethatex-
plodesunderwateratapresetdepth!TheyusedtheminWWIItoattackJa
panesesubmarines."

While Butch and Murph bickered as usual, the rest of us scram-
bled out of that pond as fast as we could and took off running. I
looked back up in the tree from my safe backyard at Murph. He was
rolling around in the tree house laughing as hard as he could. He
had fooled us all, but somehow, someway, mark my words, we
would get him back for it!

Yup, it was time to figure out how to really initiate the new kid,
and I knew just how to do it. I called a secret meeting of the
Brotherhood, this time without letting Murph know about it.

CHAPTER TWENTY-SIX
A Dare-Off To End All!

I tried really hard to convince everyone that we needed to do a dare-off on Murph and that it had to be about the crazy old lady up on the hill, but they outvoted me and we decided on something different. We were having our special meeting in my bedroom so just in case Murph came looking for us, we could hide out.

When Dad started coming up the stairs, we all stopped whispering.

"Summertime and the living is easy...," Dad always sings.

He popped his head into my bedroom. "Hello, gents."

"HI, MR. PETERS!"

All of my friends said it at the same time.

"What's up in here?" Dad saw the three candles burning on my dresser. "Oh, a Secret Brotherhood meeting, eh? Sorry to intrude. I just thought you all might need a soda, and maybe some of these?" Dad handed me a six-pack of cold cola and a huge handful of Chunky bars.

"That's okay, Dad, and thanks!"

My dad eased my door shut and left us all in my darkened bedroom.

"Your dad is the coolest ever!"

I started passing the Chunky bars out like they were playing cards.

"I wish I had your dad," Butch said.

"He even knows what we call the club, cool!" Tony slurped his soda.

Andy didn't say a word about how cool my dad was. His

dad was having some trouble again, I guess. Mom had heard about it at the CUTe & CURL, where all the ladies go to get their hair fixed up and to talk about everyone else's business. I thought that was really too bad about Andy's dad, because I have seen it with my own eyes what a fun guy he can be.

It was starting to get dark. If we were going to do something about the dare-off, we would have to get to it before dinner.

The Brotherhood decided we were going to try to set a record for the *Guinness World Book of Records**. We threw a bunch of ideas around about how we would do it.

"Why don't we see who can stand near the train tracks the longest before chickening out when a train is coming?" Tony offered.

"That's the most ridiculous thing I ever heard. What kind of a record is that? First guy to get run over is the loser? I'm not standing there with a train coming. " I said.

"How b-b-bout the l-longest loogie c-c-contest?" Andy chimed in.

"What? How would we do that? Who would measure that?"

"Well, how bout we..."

"HerecomesknowitallKeithMurphy!" Butch said purposely, running his words together like Murph did when he was talking about war stuff.

Butch was the scout for the club in this meeting, and was actually watching out for our older brothers.

He then said in the loudest whisper I have ever heard, "YO, EVERYONE HIT THE DECK. The enemy is marching..."

Tony sneered at Butch, "Heck, I like Murph, give him a break. He kind of grows on you."

"Yeah, like a fungus," Butch sneered with a chuckle.

"Yeah, th-there's a f-f-fungusam-mungus, " Andy snorted.

"Hey, you hear about Peg the one-legged dog?" Tony chuckled.

"SHHHH!" We all said as softly as we could, and ducked down as low as possible in my bedroom.

The doorbell rang and we all froze. We must have sat there holding our breath for an hour when footsteps came up the stairs and then the creaking sound of my door opening. Murph stood there with a cold can of soda and a Chunky bar in his hand.

"Peters,yourdad'sthebest!"

Everyone's eyes darted around the room trying to decide how to handle this intrusion. Technically Murph was in the Secret Brotherhood of Boys, but he hadn't been initiated yet, and that is where the dare-off was going to come in.

Well, as it turns out, it didn't take long for Murph to start strategizing and coming up with ideas that sounded like war tactics. Little did he know that the more his idea grew, the more he was going to have to do!

Butch laughed, "Geez Murph, that's not bad. Actually it's

---

*Guinness World Book of Records : the most fascinating book, detailing the feats and accomplishments of people in the strangest and most normal endeavors.

a good idea, we could do that. No one else has done that, have they, Gabe?"

I couldn't believe my ears, Butch was actually throwing a compliment Murph's way, or was he just egging him on to make the dare-off harder and thus backfiring on Murph? I pulled out my paperback *Guinness World Book of Records* and started flipping pages.

"I've read this whole book ten times cover to cover, and I don't remember ever seeing that. This really could put us in the book! Or maybe I am going to write my own book and call it the *Gabriel World Book of Records!*"

Then we all thought if we followed Murph's plan we might all get arrested and end up in juvie, like his brother. We were brave, but we weren't stupid, so we voted on his idea, and decided to do the second best idea instead, which had been one Andy and I had actually cooked up one night while sleeping out in my tent.

A loud commotion was going on out in the hall. My door was cracked open, and I could see Carl and three of his dumb friends trudging into his bedroom.

"Yo Butch, I thought you were supposed to be on lookout?" I called.

Butch just shrugged.

The big brothers were making fun of our club, standing in the hall now right outside of my door.

"Hey guys, let's light a candle and gossip like a bunch of little girls at a slumber party..." Carl sneered.

"Yeah, let's make some big plans to change our own diapers!" Carl's dumb friend Kevin added.

"NO, NO, get this, we should have a clubhouse where we all take turns talking about how macho our big brothers are and that we are just a bunch of little plebus turds..." Greg scoffed.

Butch mouthed, "Plebus turds?"

The rest of us just rolled our eyes and shrugged. We didn't care.

I stood up to close my door tight, then I heard my brother

say in a low voice, "Let's go fishing down at the lake!" All the other boys chimed in with a huge, "YEAH!"

Then Carl whispered way too loud, "My brother left a ton of night crawlers in the fridge, so we don't even have to dig any before we go!"

They all started to head downstairs and it took both Andy and Butch to hold me back when I wanted to go save my prized night crawlers from the older dorky brothers.

This would work out perfectly, though. We changed locations for the dare-off. We had thought that we would have had to do our plan from our brothers' "secret fort," but at the lake would be even better. We all got ready to go.

So the Dare-off was going to happen down at the lake, and it was going to be a dangerous one that could totally backfire. By the time we got in position, it was getting pretty dark, which was going to be awesome because what we had planned would be even better if the big brothers couldn't see who was doing what.

I had been dared to do something to my big brother and his friends that would make them so mad they might really beat me up. I dreaded the thought of what would happen to me if stupid Carl caught me. It was actually a double dare-off this time, meaning that Tony, Andy and I had come up short on the decision criteria.

Tony and Andy were up in the cave in the cliffs waiting for the right moment. The dare was for them to throw some lit firecrackers down into the boat where my brother and their big brothers were presently fishing. I had brought a couple handfuls of both the Black Cats and the Ladyfingers.

If it worked out right, the boat would drift right to the edge of the lake where the water wasn't deep and with their combined weight, they would fall out and get soaked. The part that could get me killed is that the first part of my job was to taunt them from the shore and get them to come after me to get them into position.

As soon as they were all down in the water, we would all run up the hill toward the old lady's house and disappear (we had a plan which would be the most dangerous part of all, because we would be hiding in her crawlspace, which you could get into through a trap door on the side of the house. We knew that because Gadfly's Grandma's house was the exact same house as the old lady's on the outside and the inside. We also knew that because one night we all snuck up there and spied on the crazy old lady through her side windows.) Then the big brothers, soaking wet, would get caught by the crazy old lady in her yard. Who knew if we would ever see any of them again?

The best part was that Murph (who didn't know all of the legends of the crazy old lady, or at least not the really bad ones) was going to go and 'ring and run' her, which meant he would have to ring and run to herdoor five to ten times. Every time she came to the door, his job was to let her see him (with a burlap bag over his head, and eyeholes to protect his identity. It was his idea to wear a disguise, something they did in some war.) and let her chase him around back, where he would disappear into the deep wood by the railroad tracks.

He would do this until she was steaming mad, and after about five times my brother and his friends, who would be chasing us, would show up in her yard. THAT WAS WHEN ALL HECK WOULD BREAKLOOSE! When the big brothers scattered because the crazy old lady would be chasing them, some of them would have to cross over Killer's yard. Who knew what that huge, ugly dog would do to them? It was scary, but mostly it was going to be really, really funny.

My second dangerous part was to run ahead of my brother and his friends to make sure they went to the right place. I can run a lot better than I used to, but some of the older brothers are really fast, so even though I wasn't letting on, I was already scared just thinking about them catching me, because my only real advantage would be that the older guys would all be soaking wet, and it had to be hard to climb a hill or a cliff in soaked, clinging pants. I had snuck a lighter that my dad uses to light his pipe with into my jeans pocket, and in the other pocket I stuffed a long string of Black Cat firecrackers (the funny part of that was that I bought them off of Carl). I was saving the Ladyfingers in case I needed them in the old lady's crawlspace to great a diversion.

All systems were go for the big dare-off. We got into position.

Just as we got ready and had our signals and everything down, Mr. Patchett came out on to his back porch. He was sitting out there forever, and none of us could make a move.

Carl and his friends were drifting right by where I was hiding in the thick weeds. They were catching a bunch of fish and hooting and hollering, all on my night crawlers, which burned me up and made me want revenge so bad. Their voices were echoing down the canyon and across the lake.

I looked up the hill where Murph had hiked, and two lights came on in the crazy old ladies' house. I flashed my flashlight twice at Murph, the signal that the big brothers were in position. He flashed back three times.

Mr. Patchett went back into his house, and it was all systems go!

Just as it looked like it was dark enough to start our plan, Andy's mom started calling him from across the gravel road, "ANDY, JOHNNY, TEDDY, DINNER! THIS IS THE THIRD TIME I HAVECALLED, AND I WON'T CALL YOU AGAIN! STAY OUT IF YOU WANT TO BE GROUNDED FOR THE REST OF THE SUMMER!"

"Oh m-m-man, I g-gotta go. D-Did anyone else hear my m-mom before?" Andy sounded kind of panicked. "Sh-she got so s-steamed the l-last time she called us in and n-no one showed. She threatened to g-ground us for the rest of the s-s-summer that t-t-time, and this time she really w-will! Specially m-me!"

Johnny must have said almost the exact same thing to Carl, who was guiding the boat. They started rowing to the other side of the canyon, away from our plan.

Then Eddie's mom called for him, then Butch's dad, and one by one the Secret Brotherhood disbanded before the fireworks had even started.

That was when Murph came running down from his secret position, yelling, "HEY, WHERE'SEVERYONEGOING?" and all hope of a secret attack was over.

Carl yelled into the dark night, "Oh, did the little girl's club have a plan? Looks like you dorks lucked out."

That was humiliating.

Back porch lights began flickering on all over Skyview, and then a whole chorus of moms were calling us all in, from the youngest to the oldest. That's when I saw Boney Murphy sitting up on a higher cliff than Murph and flicking a flashlight on and off. It was pointed right at his face, and he had been watching all of us. He looked like the crazy old lady's gargoyle, and that sent a big shiver up my spine.

A bunch of mom's voices echoed from the neighborhood each time with a bit more urgency. I started running toward home when I heard my own mom's voice.

All that planning had made me very hungry, and pretty soon the scent of barbecuing hamburgers, ribs and chicken legs from the backyards I passed by were making my mouth water. Carl caught up with me and ran along with me smiling, "BEAT YA HOME, CHICKEN-SLOWPOKE!"

He took off running as fast as he could, and so did I. The amazing thing was that even though he beat me home, he had a head start and he only beat me by about ten yards.

He took off running as fast as he could, and so did I. The amazing thing was that even though he beat me home, he had a head start and he only beat me by about ten yards.

Next summer, things would be different.

After all, like Dad always says, "Tomorrow is another day."

Up on the hill lives old crazy Katie. We call her Grizelda, the weirdo old lady. Don't ever go near her or you will be her lunch. So when we go by there, we huddle up in a bunch!

EPILOGUE

Many years after the previous events unfolded, Carl and I would talk long distance of the events that occurred in our childhoods. The tone of his voice made me realize that he missed me and I him.

We decided that we had enjoyed spending time together so much at our family reunion the previous summer that we ought to try to get together once a summer, every summer. We decided to meet at a camping spot Dad used to take us all the time when we were teenagers.

My sons and I were staking our tent and setting up the camp when Carl rolled up in his big black truck with my two nephews and little niece in a big roll of mountain dust.

"Nice entry, little bro!"

"Hey thanks, I thought you'd like that!" My brother stepped out and gave me a big bear hug. "Like the new wheels?"

"Sure, looks a lot like your last truck, though. Hey, pretty Nicky!"

My niece wrapped her little arms around my waist and gave me a huge hug, "I go by Nicole now, Uncle Gabe."

Then my nephews joined in for a good head rub. At the same

time, my brother was administering his own to my boys. Then the kids started throwing gear out of the back of the truck.

Carl jumped up from where he was sitting on a log near the campfire site. "Yo, Gabe, you aren't going to believe what Ryan found in our basement. Check it out!"

He carried a bundle to where I was standing, and dropped it at my feet. He started to untie, and then to unroll, an old friend.

"Oh my gosh, you still have this?" I gasped when I saw my old tent.

"Yeah, Dad gave it to me the year I moved out. Remember the summer my buddies and me drove the whole west coast? We slept in this old relic for two weeks up at Patrick's Point in Northern Cal. It's been in the basement for years."

"Man, how many times did we sleep out in this good old tent?"

"Thousands, literally. I mean, think about it. We started sleeping out in the backyard when we were just little kids. Well, I did, at least; you usually would chicken out and go sleep in Mom and Dad's room."

"Yeah, right!"

Our kids had been asking to go camping with the cousins, so there we were, up in the forest for a long weekend. We set up the old backyard tent, and set the cots in.

I lay on my back and the scent of the old tent took me back a couple decades. I felt like I was in fourth grade again. I could see the faces of the old Secret Brotherhood bustling in for a meeting, and my eyes filled at the warm memories. Oh, sometimes how I missed being a boy.

After we got our camp all set up, we went for a hike and we fished on the river. The kids had so much fun, and they each fell in at least one time - according to Nicky, some were pushed. As we were walking back to our campsite, I yelled, "Hey all, gather round, I have to tell you something really exciting!"

"What's up, Uncle Gabriel?"

"Yeah, Dad, what's going on?"

"I have a little surprise for you all when we get back to camp."

We were only about a quarter of a mile away from camp.

"WHAT IS IT?" all of them said at the same time.

"Run ahead and see! Who can get there first?"

All of a sudden they were all scrambling and holding each other back, yelling, "I'll beat you all!"

"Yeah, right, pipsqueak, I don't think so!"

"Ow, you stepped on my toe!"

"MOVE IT, SLOWPOKE!" the kid's voices echoed through the forest. We certainly weren't going to sneak up on any animals.

I jogged along behind them. Carl looked at me curiously, a bit out of breath. "What's up?"

"Oh, you'll see."

Then we heard the kids all shouting in a chorus, "GRANDPA!"

As Carl and I came through the woods into the clearing, Dad stood there smiling, surrounded by five grandchildren who were threatening to drag him to the ground and smothering him with hugs and kisses.

Carl and Dad hadn't seen each other for a year. Carl's eyes seemed to flood a little bit. He sniffled and hugged Dad really hard. I joined them, and for about fifteen seconds we all just stood in the woods in a human bear hug. As we broke up, Carl looked at me and slapped me a high five.

"GOOD MOVE, LITTLE BROTHER! YOU ALWAYS WERE THE THINKER IN THE FAMILY!"

"THAT'S FOR SURE!" I agreed, and swatted at Carl's head.

Dad showed the kids how to whittle a point with the pocketknives he brought for each of them. Each one had one of their names engraved on the side.

Carl and I fried the fish we caught, and cooked up a bunch of fried potatoes. The kids were finding long sticks for hot dogs and marshmallows, which they then whittled in a circle with their new knives.

Later, after the hot dogs and friend potatoes were gone, we all gathered around the campfire to roast marshmallows, and my nephew said, "Hey, Uncle Gabe, do you have any good scary campfire stories?"

"Oh man, do I? As a matter of fact..."

The fire reflected on Carl's suddenly frightened-looking face. Nicky huddled close to Grandpa.

"One time in this very wood, there was a hairy, scary..."

"Uh, maybe a different one," Carl said, and pointed with his eyes at little Nicky, err, Nicole. I thought to myself, hmmm, maybe someone else is still a little scared of that one.

"How about the ghost Indian in the lake story?" one of my sons asked.

Carl frowned, "You want anyone to sleep tonight? Do you plan on staying up with scared kids?"

"Scared *kids*, huh?" I said under my breath.

"Come on, Dad, we aren't going to be scared!" the kids begged.

"Yeah, my dad's stories aren't that scary, Uncle Carl!"

"Okay, well then, I'm pulling out the big guns here..."

I paused for effect. "In this very forest, not so long ago, lived *The Man in The Woods*..."

"Seriously, Gabe, that one is way too scary for certain people," Carl interrupted again.

"Are you chicken, big brother?" I teased.

"As a matter of fact, I am. How about the time we found that dead raccoon on the railroad instead?"

"Oh, yeah. Wow, I haven't thought of that for years..."

I thought for a moment about how to start it right.

'One night when we were playing hide-n-seek - me and Uncle Carl - and..."

After Dad and the kids went to the huge tent Dad had brought with him, Carl and I sat around the campfire watching the wood burn. Big CRACKS and POPS would send a piece of charred wood flying, and the low murmuring sound of Dad half-heartedly telling the kids to go to sleep and their giggling in response drew a smile from both me and Carl.

I suddenly remembered the nights that Dad would come in and tell us a bedtime story, his face even with mine since I was on the upper bunk. I missed Mom a lot at that moment, and as my eyes trailed along with a shooting star.

Memories are a strange thing. No matter how good, they can still make even a grown man homesick for a life that has passed on by.

I fed the fire, and the flames grew again, licking the air. Carl whittled on a stick, whistling something I vaguely remembered, and I could tell he was lost in another place as well. I looked at how time had changed his face as the orange reflection from the fire danced on his face.

"Hey Carl, remember when you told me the last time we were together that I ought to write down some of the old stories from the neighborhood from my old diaries?"

"Uh, yeah?"

"Well, I've been looking at the old journals, and there's some pretty funny stuff in there."

"Yeah, like what?"

I started telling him about the stories I was working on for my creative writing class to complete next semester based on our boyhood experiences. When I mentioned Gran, we went off in ten different directions. It was funny how different we both saw her.

Then the memories and stories started to come!

"Remember that time Andy's dad took us to the sand dunes with that cool dune buggy?"

"Remember when Boney Murphy came back from Chicago with poison ivy all over his face?"

"Hey, whatever happened to Murph?"

"Oh yeah, and how bout the time...."

We went on like that until my eyelids started getting really heavy. "I thinnnnk I might sleeeep..." I jumped, startled, realizing I had fallen asleep for a moment, "here by the fire toniii..."

Carl started to laugh. "Hey, you're falling asleep mid-sentence. Maybe we should turn in."

"Nah, I'm okay. I jusssss..."

Words collided, and I just couldn't keep my eyes open any longer.

"Yeah right..." Carl waited for me to respond, but I just couldn't. "Goodnight, chicken-buddy."

We had decided for old time's sake that the two of us would share the old tent with the same cots we slept on as boys, but at that moment with the full moon overhead, a slight piney breeze and the warmth of the fire, I simply couldn't move out of my chair.

"All right buddy, I'm going to hit it,' Carl said. "If you come in, I will be in the cot on the right. Don't fall on top of me!"

As he shuffled toward our tent I heard him say in a low voice, "I love you, little brother."

"I love you too," I thought, but was too tired to say it out loud.

Dear Reader,

The outpouring of letters, emails and comments about the first book in this series, Go Ask Mom - Stories from the Upper Bunk, kept the fuel burning for me while I was writing this book. What a reader feels when they connect to an author's words means more to the author than you can know.

When I endeavored to create the characters in these books, I did so with the pure intention to simply entertain. Yet somehow through my simple intentions in the first book in this series, some wonderful results have arisen.

There are bullies who bully less. Bullied kids who stand up against the bullies. Kids who were ashamed to talk about abuse taking place in their homes are getting some help, and as I understand it, some enjoyable bedtime and daytime reading taking place as a result of Gabriel Peters and his friends and family. I plan to continue to write about them, and would love to hear your impressions. Often what a reader wants snakes into the writer's head and helps hone the stories so that they are better.

I wanted this book to mostly be about friendships and how important it is to stand with a friend when he or she is going through a tough time. Please go to my website (www.justinmatott.com) to learn more about what is coming for these characters, as well as what is happening in my other writings.

As I write this I am outlining the third and fourth book in this series. Gabriel's crazy grandma is going to come to stay, and of course with a character like that, everything is bound to be just a bit different going forward. The working title for the third book is The Gabriel World Book of Records, in which he and his buddies endeavor to get in the famous Guinness book - and you can just imagine what they are going to attempt, including the World's Largest Spit Pool.

Thank you for reading my books and stay tuned. In book three Gabriel is going into fifth grade finally, and yes, finally he really is going to switch schools. No more Batwomen, but this book will have its own set of issues and adventures Gabriel is going to have to overcome and learn, just like you and me.

Yours truly,

Justin Matott

June 22, 2008

rankenstein and [...]
and the Werewolf are my [...]
When the fifty foot woman attac[...]
These three will just defend
The fifty foot woman is just like her
S.M.C is a fiend so big and hairy
So someday me and my monster friends
Will make her nighttime scary

THIS ONE COULD GET ME KI[...]

Carl and Denise were kissing
When they locked down deep on Halloween
They locked their braces good and tight
Oh what a funny scene
Carlio is in love
She makes him get all mushy
I hear them talking on the phone
Carl says stuff really gushy
Like no I like the way you comb your hair
Well I kind of liked that movie
But the funniest thing was when h[...]
said
I think you're really groovy

Dear Grandma,
I know you don't like mushy
stuff, but I wanted to tell you
how important you are. When
I come to see you my heart
dances like your favorite guy
Freddy Astare. I think you are
terrific and I am glad you are
my grandma, a lot.
Love,
Gabe

to do something
[...]g in the world record
[...] what will do? I just
[...] don't know Mr. Guinness
to make [...]
take a look.

A dumb poem I have to write for class
this is my practice stuff

Green is grass and green is puke, I [...]
grass, it's the color of S.M.C skin th[...]
get too close

Brown is dirt and brown is poop, [...]
up I wish I could turn in this p[...]
get in trouble (again)

Red is a bully's face, they look [...]
if a bully gets really mad will [...]

Black is my brother's broken [...]
rake he howled and cried whi[...]
think it was all fake (beca[...]
him to the Dairy Queen [...]
got to go and get a swirl [...]
should pop himself in the [...]

White is the snow,
white is a cloud.
white is so very pret[...]
there is no white to [...]
in a big old grimy ci[...]
(I should know mor[...]
on the street was [...]

My grandma is a looney
tune
But man she makes me
giggle
She is the funniest
person I know
And her stories make me
wiggle

A man
dissolves
and
nozi[...]

[...]dy is my best friend
[...] all
He is funny and fun I
think
So how can I tell my
bestest friend
Hey Andy your breath
just stinks !!!

5. Cat[...]
tun[...]
bett[...]

6 [...]

Sawyer is a crazy guy
He jumped off the monster
high
I never thought I'd see the day
That Sawyer would ever cry
But broken bones will do that
[...]